BUG OFF!

Also by Terri Fields:

The Day the Fifth Grade Disappeared
Fourth-Graders Don't Believe in Witches

BUG OFF!

TERRI FIELDS

AN
APPLE
PAPERBACK

SCHOLASTIC INC.
New York Toronto London Auckland Sydney

ISBN 0-590-48941-0

Copyright © 1995 by Terri Fields.
All rights reserved. Published by Scholastic Inc.
APPLE PAPERBACKS is a registered trademark of Scholastic Inc.

12 11 10 9 8 7 6 5 4 3 2   5 6 7 8 9/9 0/0

Printed in the U.S.A.   40

First Scholastic printing, February 1995

*In Thanks to Donna Lynn Cook,
a most magical sister*

*and love always to
Rick, Lori, Jeff, Janet Fields,
and Barbara Bernstein*

BUG OFF!

1

"**I** hate my little brother! I hate him! I hate him!" My mother doesn't ever want me to say that, but it's true, and so I'm saying it anyway. Since I'm already in my room and I'm already grounded, I don't see how it's going to get me in any more trouble. Besides, it feels great to yell the words at the top of my voice.

The thing about my little brother is that he's a total and complete jerk. He's seven years old and he gets worse every year. Somehow, though, he's got Mom fooled. When she's around, he plays the I'm-just-the-poor-little-picked-on-innocent-kid part real well. A perfect example is the way I'm in my room grounded today, when he should be the one getting punished.

Actually, it probably doesn't matter if I have to stay in my room forever, because after what my dear little brother Tyler did, I'll probably be too embarrassed to ever go to school again anyway.

It feels like I've been in my room for days, so I can't believe this whole mess just started after school today. When I got home, I noticed that a bunch of the guys from the fifth grade were playing touch football next door on Jason's front lawn. I also saw that one of them just happened to be Jeff, the cutest boy in the whole class. He's new to our school, and like every other girl in our class, I really wish Jeff would notice me. So with all the guys next door, I figured that it couldn't hurt to change into my leggings and new sweater and matching socks I had gotten for my birthday. Then I could just happen to wander outside in my front yard, and if Jeff just happened to notice me, well . . . great!

I ran upstairs to my bedroom to change real fast. I pulled my new long purple sweater over my head and put on my black leggings. Then I yanked open my underwear drawer to get my new purple socks. But there, right in my drawer, was this awful-looking snake curled up in the middle of all my underwear and socks. It looked like it was about to bite me. I screamed as loud as I could; then I pulled out my drawer, ran to the window, and threw the drawer and the snake right out the window. Thank goodness I got rid of the drawer before the snake bit me, but I was so scared that I was still standing at the window shaking and screaming when my mother and my little brother ran into my room.

"Good heavens, Krista, what's the matter?" my mother called, looking frantic.

"There's . . . there's . . ." My voice was coming in gasps; I could hardly get the words out. "There's this big, awful, terrible snake in my drawer. I think it was a rattlesnake. It was all curled up, and it was ready to bite me. I was so scared . . . I just . . ."

I was interrupted by a giggle, and I looked at my dear little brother, who was biting his lip to keep from laughing louder. Mom put her hands on her hips. "Tyler, do you have something to say?"

"Geez, Mom, it was only a little rubber snake! How come she got so scared over one dumb little rubber snake?" His blue eyes looked at her innocently, but Mom didn't seem to be buying this one.

"Tyler, it was not necessary or nice to put any snake in your sister's drawer, fake or not. You have to respect her privacy."

Tyler looked at the floor and then got that pretend-sorry look on his face. "I traded Bobby Johnson two Hot Wheels cars for that snake, and I just wanted to share it with Krista. I didn't know she would think it was real; even the first-graders didn't think that dumb snake was real."

Mom ran a hand through her hair, "Well, Tyler, your sister did think it was real. It was nice of you to want to share with her, but that was not the best way to do it. Now, first you apologize to her." Mom looked out my window at the mess below and sighed. "Next, you go downstairs, get Krista's drawer and all the things that belong in it, and then you bring everything back up to your sister."

Tyler looked at me, and his eyes said he was glad I'd fallen for the snake. "I'm sorry," he mumbled.

"You are not!" I said. "Mom, he isn't sorry at all. Just look at his face."

"Krista, he apologized. He will return all of your things to you. Now, just let it go."

I folded my arms in front of me. Why was it when I did something I got a huge, long lecture about being the oldest, and when he did something, he got off with one tiny, little, dumb, unmeant apology? "I don't even want him touching my stuff. I'll go get it myself," I said. "Just tell him he can't be in my room anymore, ever again."

My mother shook her head. "You two. I'm so tired of this fighting. Tyler, stay out of Krista's room. Krista, stop making such a big deal out of everything. Now, will the two of you be quiet; I'm trying to finish a report for work tomorrow."

I stormed down the stairs, pulled open the front door, walked outside to retrieve my underwear, and froze. I had totally forgotten about Jeff and all the boys from school playing football next door. Besides, they weren't exactly playing football anymore. They were kind of standing in a circle around Tyler's rubber snake . . . and all my underwear. What was I supposed to do? I did not want to leave those boys there with all my stuff, but there was no way in the entire world that I was going to walk over to them and start picking all my underwear up in front of them. I wanted to die right there and right then. But almost like a slow-motion thing in the movies, the boys looked up from my pile of stuff and saw that I was outside. I could feel my face getting hot. I could feel my heart pounding so hard that it was about to pop out of my chest. Somewhere inside me, some voice that didn't even sound like mine croaked, "Go away! Just go away! This isn't even your house."

I was so embarrassed that my ears started to ring, and I didn't even hear what the boys said. All I know is that they went back to Jason's. I think I heard them laughing, but my ears were barely hearing. I waited until they were gone before I ran onto the lawn, stepped over Tyler's dumb rubber snake, threw all my stuff in my drawer, and rushed back into the house.

Running up the stairs, I could feel the tears

splashing down my cheeks. Jeff had certainly noticed me. I could only imagine what he and his friends were saying. I would be the class joke. I dropped the drawer in my room and headed for Tyler's room. I walked in, grabbed him, and pushed him onto the floor. "You are such a jerk! I can't believe you did this to me!"

I sat on top of Tyler to hold him down. At ten and a half I was a lot taller and stronger than my little brother. The next thing I knew, my mother was there pulling me off Tyler. "*Now*, what's going on?"

"All the boys from school were outside, and . . . and there was all of my under — "

Tyler began to whisper, "I see London, I see France . . ." and something just snapped. I grabbed Tyler's hair and pulled it as hard as I could. He screamed.

"Krista, that's enough. Go to your room!"

"Me? *Me* go to my room? Punish Tyler. He's the one who's been — "

My mother interrupted. "Look, I don't have time for this. I have got to finish my report." My mother was still dressed in her gray business suit and high heels. "Tyler should not have been in your room. However, he has apologized for that. He certainly could not have known that you would think his snake was real, and he most certainly could not have known that you would throw your

6

things out the window or that anyone else would have been there to see them."

"But Mom, you don't understand, all those boys — "

Mom interrupted, "Honey, calm down. This isn't the end of the world. Those boys didn't see anything from your drawer that they don't see every time they go into the department store."

"But that stuff in the store isn't mine. How can you say it's the same thing? If Tyler was upset, you would care. Tyler's always right; I'm always wrong. I hate him! I hate him!"

"Krista," my mother had that warning voice that mothers get, but I was too mad to hear it. "I want you to calm down, act your age, and stop saying you hate your little brother."

All I could think of was that the next day I would have to face Jeff and all the other guys in the fifth grade. "I do hate my brother!" I stamped my foot. "And . . . if you can't understand why, then . . . then . . . I hate you, too!"

So that's why I'm sitting in my room, grounded. But I know what I'm going to do. I'm going to take out my special book, a kind of diary that my grandma sent me last month. I've been using it to keep track of the reasons I hate my little brother. I was going to write down every awful thing he did, but then I decided that if I did that, my entire diary would have been filled up in just one day. Besides, my hand would have ached a lot, so I've only been putting in the very worst stuff Tyler does. Even so, I've already written four unbelievably disgusting "Tyler things," and today is definitely going down as the fifth reason why I hate my little brother.

2

That night I had awful dreams about having to face the boys in my class. At five in the morning, I decided that the only way for me to survive this mess was to stay away from school for a while, then maybe the boys would sort of forget about me — and my flying underwear. It wasn't a great idea, but it was the best idea I could think of, so when Mom came to wake me, I told her I was feeling pretty sick, and maybe I should stay home. Mom was staring at me with one of those I'm-not-at-all-sure-if-I-believe-you looks, and I was doing my best to look as sick as I could. I was doing such a good job that I almost felt as if I had a fever. I groaned softly, and I could tell Mom was almost ready to let me stay home when Tyler stuck his head in the door of my room.

"How come Krista gets to stay in bed? Can I stay home, too? I want to watch *Star Trek*. Please, please? It's Krista's and my favorite show, and the ones we like are only on when we're in school, huh, Krista?"

Mom put her hand on my forehead. Then she looked at me and then at Tyler. "I think you'd both better try going to school today. If you don't feel well later, you can call me at work."

"But Mom . . ." My voice was desperate.

"Krista, get up and get ready. You, too, Tyler. Get going, so I can drop you both off at school on my way to work." The tone in her voice said that there was no use pleading because she wasn't going to change her mind. Once again, my wonderful little brother had messed up my life!

I pulled on a pair of jeans and a baggy, faded-blue sweatshirt. Maybe I could just fade into the walls enough at school so that no one would even notice I was there. Just as I was combing my hair, Tyler stuck his head in the door of my room. "I almost had Mom letting us stay home from school, huh, Krista?" He looked so proud of himself.

My mouth dropped open. "You . . . you almost what? Oh . . . go away!" I sighed real, real deeply. Why couldn't I be an only child like my best friend Julia?

My life was about to turn into a complete and total disaster. "Mom," I pleaded as I sat in the car, "I just can't go to school today after what Tyler did. Please don't make me."

"Oh, Krista," she said, honking as she passed

a slow driver on her left. "No one will even remember. Now stop making such a big deal out of it."

"Hey, I had to go all the way downstairs and look through the grass to get my snake back. Mom, Krista threw away my snake."

He was just unbelievable. I had to have the world's worst luck in brothers, but I couldn't worry about that now. I was getting desperate. School was only a few blocks away, and I knew I would not — could not — go inside Horizon Elementary School today. Then it hit me; I didn't have to! When Mom dropped us off, she was always in a big hurry to get to work; she usually pulled away as soon as she let us out of the car. All I had to do was wave good-bye, let Tyler go ahead of me, and then, after he got into the building, I could just sneak back home. I smiled. Maybe things weren't going to be a total disaster. At least I would have a whole day without school *or* Tyler.

For once, I was almost glad that Tyler was jabbering away to Mom; it gave me time to think out my plan. By the time we were in front of the school I had it all figured out. Tyler was still blabbering on, ". . . and Mommy, I have one more favorite show. I'll tell you about that one, too. It's *Leave It to Beaver*. It's real old, but it's neat. See, on the last show, the Beav decided he would sneak back home from school and watch TV. His daddy dropped him off at the school, but the Beav . . . well, he hadn't done his homework, and he didn't want to get in trouble, so he walked real slow to the school doors until his daddy's car left the school, and then . . ."

I couldn't believe what I was hearing! Of all the TV shows in the world, why did he have to choose that one to explain to Mom at this moment? I could only hope that Mom tuned Tyler out as much as I did. The car pulled up at Horizon, and Mom handed each of us a sack lunch, but then, instead of pulling away like she did every other day, Mom watched from her car until we'd both walked through the front door of the school. So much for my sneaking home. Tyler, the brat, had done it again. Now he was reading my mind. Great. Just great.

"Bye, Krista," Tyler called as he turned toward Mrs. Maland's second-grade classroom. He waved and smiled with a grin that said he was so proud his top front tooth had fallen out. I totally ignored him and walked quickly into Mrs. Kendall's class. I slunk into the classroom, quietly slid into my seat, and pretended to be doing some math homework. That's when I saw Jeff walk into the classroom. My heart was pounding, and my hand was shaking. Why did he have to be so cute! He had a great smile and the neatest brown eyes. Jeff went to his seat, and didn't say a word. I began

12

to think that maybe my mom was right. Maybe no one was going to say anything.

Jason, Sean, and Matt ran in just as the tardy bell was ringing, and since Mrs. Kendall did NOT like tardies, they practically flew to their seats. The morning announcements ended, and math started. Each time one of the boys walked by my desk, I looked at the floor and waited for the teasing to start. But somehow, miracle of miracles, the whole day passed without the boys saying anything to me at all. During science, I noticed them whispering to each other and got really worried, but then I overheard them at recess. Jason said, "I don't care *what* you think. I said it in science, and I'll say it again. The Mets will win the pennant."

Matt started to argue, and I quit listening when I realized they weren't talking about me at all, they were just talking about baseball. What a relief!

By the time school was over I was really tired. My head hurt, my stomach hurt. It had been an awful day, but it could have been a lot worse. At least I knew that the underwear incident was not going to be the major gossip of the school!

I was so relieved that I barely minded walking Tyler home from school. Mom didn't want him walking by himself, and she said that I could walk home with my friends if I wanted, but Tyler had to tag along. Sometimes, Julia or Michelle walked almost all the way home with me, but lots of the time, they got sick of waiting for Tyler to kick a rock, and they started out with us and then walked ahead. I didn't really blame them. Every day I yelled at Tyler to hurry up, and every day he paid no attention. Today, as we left school, I thought about telling Julia and Michelle the snake and underwear story. But it was over — why bring it up again?

Tyler found a rock, and, as usual, every time it went too far in one direction or the other, he had to bring it back and start kicking it again. I had complained to Mom over and over about how slow he was, but she always said, "How much more time can it take if he wants to kick a rock home? Besides, if Tyler's busy, he isn't interfering with you and your friends."

So while I watched Tyler kick his rock, Michelle turned to me and said, "Krista, we're going to have to go ahead of you today because I've got a makeup dance lesson, and Julia's got her piano lesson." Then she looked at Tyler inching his way home and shook her head. "Maybe one day he'll be a great football kicker, and we'll tell people that we knew him when he was just a little kid who kicked rocks."

I groaned, "I don't think he's ever going to be anything but a great big pain."

Julia giggled. "He looks like such a sweet little kid, the kind that old ladies love to just pinch on the cheek."

"Yeah, but we know better!" I added. My friends agreed with me and waved good-bye. "Come on, Tyler. Leave the stupid rock, and let's go home!"

He ignored me and kicked the rock again. It rolled in front of my foot, and I walloped it. It flew into some bushes. "Now," I said, "it's gone. Let's just go home!" But Tyler began looking around for another rock, found one, and began kicking it.

When we finally got home, after what seemed like hours, there was a message from Mom on the answering machine saying that she had to stay at work until 5:30 and for us to call her if we needed her. Usually, my mom worked at the office while we were at school, and at her computer at home when we were home, but if a client needed her she worked late once in a while. As moms went she was pretty neat, except for this blind spot she had when it came to Tyler. She was always defending him — even when he should have gotten in trouble. I think, maybe, it had something to do with my dad. Everyone said that Tyler looked just like him. He had been killed in a car accident a few years back. I was just about Tyler's age when it happened, and Tyler was just a baby. I sort of remember that night — waiting for dad to come home, but he didn't . . . I could feel my eyes filling up with tears.

The doorbell rang, and I was glad because I still didn't like to think too much about my dad and what had happened. I heard Tyler answer the door, and then a few minutes later, he yelled for me. I ran down the stairs and there, standing on my front steps were Jason, Matt, Sean, and Jeff. "Hi," Jason said grinning. "We heard you were quite a pitcher, and we want to ask you to join our baseball team."

I wasn't sure what was going on. I mean I was really glad Jeff was there, but I wasn't a pitcher. Suddenly, I noticed that Jason, Matt, Sean, and Jeff were wearing boxer shorts over their jeans, and my face must have turned bright red because Jason laughed and said, "Tyler explained to us that it was you who threw the drawer out the window — we're sure you could be our star pitcher. See, we even wore uniforms that we're going to call Krista's undercover specials!"

Tyler smiled, "Yeah, Krista. The guys didn't know why your underwear was all over the front yard, but I told 'em. I told 'em that you stood at the window and you threw the drawer real, real far on the front lawn." Tyler looked so proud of himself. "I get to be your team's water boy. Jason says so, but I don't think I wanna wear your uniforms."

Jason laughed even harder. "Awww, Tyler. It's just that our boxers don't have flowers, like Krista's underwear, but we can work on that."

I ran back in the house and slammed the door. Jason was obnoxious, but most fifth-grade boys were, and every fifth-grade girl had to deal with them. But the thing that was so unfair — so impossible — was having a little brother like Tyler to go along with everything else. *No* fifth-grade girl should have to deal with that!

3

I still had not spoken to Tyler when my mother got home. I couldn't wait to tell her what he had done. She'd been so sure that everything would work out okay today, and it had, sort of, until Tyler had opened his big mouth. Boy was Tyler going to get in lots of trouble.

Just as I started to say "Guess what, Mom?" I saw that her briefcase was bulging, and she looked real tired. I decided maybe I should wait a few minutes so she could really listen to everything. That way she could get super mad at Tyler.

"Hi, Krista, honey." She put her briefcase down and sighed. "Gee, I was hoping you might have already set the table."

At that moment, Tyler walked in the kitchen, "Mommy, you're home! I missed you. I kept telling Krista that we should make dinner for you, but she wouldn't even talk to me. I was going to make you an ice-cream-and-cookie sandwich!"

Mom hugged Tyler and laughed. "Oh, honey, I

love you. It's been such a rotten day, and you make Mommy so happy." I rolled my eyes. That kid. "Tell you what, we'll have the cookie-and-ice-cream sandwich some other day. Tonight, I think we'll just have pizza." Mom dialed Pizza Hut, and while she waited for them to answer, she began leafing through the address book on her desk. "Krista, did you like Mrs. Mulroom?"

"She was an all-right baby-sitter, why?" I asked.

"Well, I've got to go out of town tomorrow. There's a large order that was misfiled, and if I don't get things calmed down in Wichita, we're going to lose a very big client. I just hate these last minute things, but no one else seems to be able to handle this one. I've got to go."

"Oh," I said. Great, not only was I not going to get to tell her about Tyler, but she was going to be gone altogether. I didn't much like it when my mom was gone. Even though I was getting older, it still felt good to know she was there when I went to sleep at night. Besides, whenever Mom was gone, Tyler was *really* a pain.

The pizza came, and I had three slices with black olives and mushrooms. When I had finished, my mom was still on the phone. I heard her talking to her best friend, Donna. "I just don't know what I'm going to do. I've tried every one of our regular sitters, and no one is available; I can't postpone this trip. I've got to go." Mom listened to Donna for a few minutes. "Well, I guess you're right. That agency does have a good reputation; I guess I'll just have to try one of their sitters."

Mom hung up and reached for the phone book. This was not a good sign. "Uhh. What are you doing, Mom?"

"Not now, Krista. I'll explain everything to you after I get it worked out."

I trudged out of the kitchen. When were things going to calm down enough so that I could explain about the boys and their boxers and Tyler? I went into the family room and turned on the TV. At least one of my favorite programs was on, but just as I started getting interested in the show, Tyler came in. "Change the channel. That's too scary."

"I will not change the channel," I said through gritted teeth. "I like this show."

"It's too scary. I don't like it."

"Then get out of here and shut up. I'm missing all the good parts."

Tyler started to cry, and Mom came in. "Kids, please, don't fight. I just can't take it tonight."

Tyler's innocent blue eyes looked up at her, "But Mommy, I'm scared, and Krista won't change the channel. I'm gonna have bad dreams tonight. Monsters are gonna come."

"Oh, for pete's sake! There aren't any monsters on this show!"

My mother's brown eyes glared at mine. "Krista, change the channel or turn off the TV! If he says this show is scaring him, it must be scaring him."

"But I was watching — "

"Krista, now!"

I sighed and changed the channel. How did the kid do it so well?!

Later that evening, after I was all ready for bed, Mom came in my room. Maybe I would finally get a chance to explain about my afternoon with Tyler.

Mom sat down on my bed and began to brush my long, curly red hair. "Krista, I'm sorry that I wasn't here this afternoon and that I've been so busy tonight. Honey, I'm going to need for you to be a really big girl for the next few days. We're going to have to have a new sitter here. I want you to help her, and I want you to take extra good care of Tyler for me. I'm counting on you."

I didn't like the sound of that at all. My mom always tried the sitters out for at least an evening before she hired them to take care of us when she went out of town. I mean, what happened if this new sitter turned out to be a real witch?

"Aren't we even going to get to meet her first?" My eyes locked into my mom's.

"I'm afraid not," my mom said. "She can't get here until after you've left for school tomorrow, but I promise you, if she doesn't seem all right to me, I won't leave. And even if she's okay, I'll make sure you have my hotel phone number. If there's anything you don't like about this sitter, you call me." Mom ran her hand through her hair, and I noticed that little streaks of gray were starting to show through the brown. "I'm sorry we didn't get to talk about your day today, but I've still got to pack, and I'm so tired. Tell you what, you take real good care of Tyler for me while I'm gone, and when I get back you and I will have a special Mom and Krista day all by ourselves, okay?"

By the time I got up the next morning, Mom had made lists and lists of stuff for the baby-sitter. She hustled Tyler and me off to school, hugging us as we got out of the car, and reminding us that she loved us both to pieces. She also told us that she would be home as soon as she could. Meanwhile, we were to behave ourselves, and we were not to fight. It was on the tip of my tongue to tell her that I was not the one who started the fights, but Mom waved again and then drove off.

When I got to Mrs. Kendall's class, I took a deep breath. There was no way of telling for sure whether Jason was finished with his little joke or just getting started. When I walked through the door, I gasped. Cassandra Smythington had dyed her hair bright pink with orange stripes. It was all anyone talked about all day long. She said she had done it because KPXN radio was giving away tickets to see Hot Striped Melon to the person with the most outrageous hair. Cassandra's older sister was going to try to get tickets, only she wasn't going to take Cassandra, so Cassandra figured she would just win her own, and that would show her big sister. Only when her mom saw what Cassandra had done, she'd grounded Cassandra for the rest of her life.

It was an awesome story, and Cassandra spent recess and our whole lunch hour describing how she'd decided on the colors and how she had gotten the stripes in. We were all so interested, that Jason never said or did anything more about my underwear. I even sort of forgot about the whole thing myself. The day went by really fast, and before I knew it, school was out, we had headed home, and Tyler had almost kicked his dumb rock the whole way. I could see Jason up ahead of us, but he didn't turn around, and I was just as glad. As we got to our street, I suddenly remembered that Mom wasn't going to be home; we were going to have some new baby-sitter from the agency.

I shifted my backpack while I thought. If I could just make it clear to this baby-sitter that Tyler was a jerk, and that he wasn't to be believed about *anything*, well, the time might turn out okay. I would just have to set things straight from the beginning before those innocent blue eyes of his went to work on her.

I walked ahead of Tyler, turning around every so often to make sure he was still headed for home. Reaching our beige stucco house, I knocked on the front door. A rather round-looking little lady with white hair and granny glasses opened it. "Come in, come in," she welcomed. "I'm Mrs. Pickle-Nickle."

"Mrs. Pickle-Nickle," I said, trying not to laugh. It almost sounded like the name of the magical character in all the books I read when I was Tyler's age. It certainly didn't sound like any real person's name.

"And you . . . you must be Krista." She continued, "I'm so glad you're home. I would love to hear about your school day, and I've just finished baking you some chocolate chip cookies."

My stomach caught the scent of those cookies, and it growled. They really did smell delicious. I followed the baby-sitter into the kitchen. She served me a plate of cookies and a large glass of milk. The rich, chocolatey cookies were the best I had ever eaten anywhere. One time Mom and I had gone to San Francisco, and we had gotten cookies from a place on the pier that said WORLD'S BEST COOKIES, but these were even better!

"I really like your pretty red curls," exclaimed Mrs. Pickle-Nickle as I ate. "I'd give anything to have my hair curl that way!"

"You would?" I said through a mouthful of cookie, and I began to think that this baby-sitter just might be okay.

There was a banging at the door. It had to be Tyler, and I hadn't even had a chance to explain about how I was in charge and he was always causing trouble. Mrs. Pickle-Nickle scurried to answer the door. I had to smile as I watched her. This lady looked like a cross between Mrs. Santa Claus and everyone's favorite television grandma. In no time, she was holding Tyler's hand and leading him to the kitchen.

"My sister didn't even wait for me, and she's supposed to," he whined. Then he smelled and saw the cookies. "Hey, how come she got the cookies first? Did she get the biggest ones?" His blue eyes looked up at Mrs. Pickle-Nickle through the patch of hair that always fell in one eye. "If you're gonna be our baby-sitter, you better know that sometimes, I can't go to sleep unless my mommy is there to tuck me in! I might have to stay up and watch cartoons instead."

Mrs. Pickle-Nickle smiled, and I noticed that she even had a dimple on either side of her smile. "Well, Tyler, I'm sure we'll get everything worked out. Now, don't you worry. I've saved a nice extra-big cookie for you."

Tyler climbed up on his chair and wolfed down the cookie. Before I could get a word in about being in charge, Tyler began explaining his day to Mrs. Pickle-Nickle. "See, I'm real good in math, and usually, I always get my math paper on the board. But today, we had to add some numbers to follow some dots and it made a picture. Then we had to color it. Ricky Golden had this really super new big crayon; it had all different colors in it, and when he colored with it, the whole picture was so great! The teacher liked Ricky's picture best, so she put it on the board. Boy, I wish, I wish super-duper-much that I could have a crayon like that! Boy, I wish more than anything that I had it right now."

I looked at Mrs. Pickle-Nickle to see if she thought Tyler was being dumb, and it was probably just the way the light bounced off her glasses or something, because it almost looked as if for a minute her hazel eyes glowed bright yellow. Anyway, she reached into the pocket of her apron and said, "You know, Tyler, I just happen to have a crayon that sounds something like the one you've described. You're welcome to it if you'd like." When she pulled her hand from her pocket, there was a fat crayon. It must have had at least twelve different colors in it.

I wondered how she happened to have a crayon just like the one Tyler wanted, but Tyler didn't worry about that. He just reached out and took the crayon. "Wow! Wow!" He turned it around and around. "Wow!" he repeated again. "This is ten times better than Ricky's, and you're really gonna let me keep it?"

"Absolutely. I'm glad you like it." Mrs. Pickle-Nickle stood up and began to clear the table of our empty cookie plates and milk glasses.

This woman was some baby-sitter. Because my mom often had business, we had had a lot of different sitters, and believe me, none of them had done as much in days as Mrs. Pickle-Nickle had done in just a few minutes. I could hardly wait to see what we had to look forward to for the rest of her stay. Still, for some dumb reason, I had a feeling that something wasn't quite right. I shrugged. It was probably just that I was already worrying that Tyler would do something else really dumb to mess up my life. And, speaking of Tyler, so much had happened since I'd gotten home from school, that I still hadn't had a chance to explain to Mrs. Pickle-Nickle that I was in charge, and she was supposed to listen only to me and never to Tyler.

4

Tyler got some paper and began to draw with his new crayon. For a few minutes the room was real quiet, then Tyler brushed his hair out of his eyes and said, "Boy, Krista, I bet you wish you had a crayon like this!"

"Oh, yeah, for sure, I really want one." I hoped he could hear the disgust in my voice.

Mrs. Pickle-Nickle came over to the table. "Krista, I think I could get another crayon if you'd like one like your brother's."

Oh great, I thought to myself. Doesn't this lady see that there is a big difference between Tyler and me? She can't possibly lump the two of us into the same category. Suddenly, I had visions of seven-thirty bedtimes, and I winced.

Tyler kept coloring, but out of nowhere, he asked, "Is tonight Thursday?"

"Why yes, I believe it is," said Mrs. Pickle-Nickle.

Tyler sighed, "I wish it was Wednesday." He

put on his I-know-all-the-important-stuff-around-here voice, and explained to Mrs. Pickle-Nickle, "You see we have to have brussels sprouts for dinner every Thursday, and I just hate 'em!"

Mrs. Pickle-Nickle thought a moment. "Do you like them, Krista?"

Well, at least my opinion counted for something. I was tempted to say that I loved brussels sprouts, just to spite Tyler. But the truth was that I hated the yucky green little balls, too. Mom was on one of her health kicks and decided that we had to have a different vegetable at least three nights a week. Thursdays were designated as brussels sprouts night. "Actually, Mrs. Pickle-Nickle, I really don't like them much myself."

Mrs. Pickle-Nickle pushed her glasses up higher onto the bridge of her nose. "Hmmm," she said, "I don't really suppose it would hurt anything if you skipped eating them just this once."

Tyler looked up from his coloring. "Wow! That's pretty neat." Then he scowled, "But it may make Mommy kinda mad. Hey! I know! Why doesn't Krista eat the brussels sprouts. Then you can tell Mommy that you made 'em. Besides, she's the oldest; she always says she should get to do stuff I don't, so she can eat brussels sprouts, and I won't!"

I wanted to kill him. I really did, but instead, I smiled sweetly at Mrs. Pickle-Nickle. "Actually,

I think it would be a good idea if Tyler ate the brussels sprouts. He's so small that they might help him grow into a normal person."

Our baby-sitter looked a little perplexed. "Maybe, we don't have to decide about the brussels sprouts just this minute. Tyler, what are you drawing?"

Tyler looked at her proudly. "It's a picture — it's a picture of Krista throwing her drawer out of her bedroom window."

Mrs. Pickle-Nickle looked even more confused. "She did what?"

"Tyler," I whispered angrily, and my brown eyes shot daggers at him that said to shut up or I was going to kill him.

Tyler shrugged, and before he could say anything else, I jumped in. "Mrs. Pickle-Nickle, you have to watch out for Tyler. He can be a little difficult." I got that exact same tone that my mom used when she wanted to talk to another adult about us.

"I am not difficult. I am just fine." He folded his arms and glared at me.

I interrupted with what I hoped was a mom-type laugh. "You have to be especially careful of his fake snake. He leaves it in the strangest places, and I wouldn't want it to scare you."

"Oh, my!" Mrs. Pickle-Nickle replied. "Well, I — "

Before she could finish, Tyler rudely jumped in, "Only a dummy would ever think that snake was really real. Besides, I don't even have it anymore. I sold it." With that, Tyler bent his head over his paper and began to color again.

I wondered if the second-grader Tyler had sold the snake to would use it to drive his big sister crazy. Probably not. I was probably the only one in the whole world "lucky" enough to get such a little brother. Well, at least, I wouldn't have to worry about the stupid thing being stuck in my bed or something. It was gone, and I was glad.

I headed out of the kitchen to stake out my spot in front of the television before Tyler claimed it when I heard Mrs. Pickle-Nickle say, "So, Tyler, I've never tried to sell a snake. Did one of your friends buy it?"

Curious, I listened for the answer. "Oh, no," he answered. "The guy who lives next door, his name is Jason, he bought it from me after school. He said he wanted to see what my sister would throw around the school. He also said something about how seeing Krista and the snake would make school lots more fun for everyone."

I wheeled around. "You jerk! You sold your snake to Jason? I can't believe you!"

Tyler looked at me. "But Jason gave me a whole dollar. Besides, if you hadn't left me to walk the rest of the way home by myself, which you aren't

31

supposed to do, I wouldn't have even talked to Jason about my snake." He folded his arms across his chest and stuck out his chin. "Plus, you better be nicer to me or else I'm gonna give Jason some of your underwear so he can hang it from the school flagpole like he wants to! So there!"

My mouth fell open. I tried to yell at Tyler, and for a minute only a kind of strange croak came out. I could feel myself getting madder and madder, and my redheaded temper was about to explode. "Ohhh! I wish . . . I just wish that you were a tiny little beetle bug, so I could step on you!"

"Oh, now, Krista," Mrs. Pickle-Nickle interrupted. "Surely, you don't mean that."

"Yes, I most certainly, definitely, for sure *do* wish it. He'd be much better as a little beetle bug than a brother." I stuck out my tongue at him. "I really wish you were a bug."

Tyler stood up on his chair. "Oh, yeah . . . well . . . well, I'd super rather be a little beetle bug than your brother. In fact, I really wish I was a beetle bug right now. Then I would crawl away somewhere too small for you to ever bother me."

"Now," Mrs. Pickle-Nickle tried to soothe, "Tyler, you wouldn't really want to be a beetle bug."

"Oh, yeah? I like beetle bugs. I don't like Krista!"

I think Mrs. Pickle-Nickle said something, but

I don't know what, because by this time, I was just inches from my little brother's face. With him standing on the chair, we were almost the same height, and we were both glaring into each other's eyes. My fists were clenched, and they were just itching to hit him. How dare he even consider helping Jason to hang my underwear from the school flagpole! My right hand just sort of reached up. I wasn't really going to hit Tyler — hard — just enough to let him know I had had it. But then something very strange happened. My hand only connected with air. Tyler wasn't there! How had he gotten off the chair without my even seeing him? Then suddenly, I heard a voice. It was kind of small and scratchy. "Hey," it called, "I feel really weird. Everything looks real different. What's going on?"

"Tyler," I said, "if that's you, and you're playing some other dumb trick, you'd better stop it right now!"

The small scratchy voice began to cry. "This isn't a trick. Something is really wrong."

I looked down in the direction from which the voice was coming. There was no one there. "Tyler, quit fooling around, and come in here now!"

"But I am here!" the voice cried. "I didn't move off the chair."

I looked carefully at the chair, but Tyler was definitely not there. In fact, there was nothing on the chair. Then I saw something little and black crawl across the seat. It was a beetle bug.

"Krista," Tyler's voice said. "Help!"

I knew it couldn't be. It just couldn't. I mean it didn't make any sense. But the voice seemed to be coming from the seat of the chair. Even though I hated bugs almost as much as I hated snakes, I leaned over the beetle bug. Feeling pretty stupid and a little scared, I whispered to the bug, "Tyler?"

"Uh-huh," the voice answered.

"Oh, no!" I gasped.

5

My knees started shaking, so I sat down on the floor before my legs gave out. My face was almost level with the chair. This could not be happening. We were a perfectly normal family. We weren't magic. We didn't believe in elves or giants, and we certainly didn't think there was such a thing as talking bugs. This beetle thing had to be a trick. But how could my dumb seven-year-old brother pull off any trick this amazing? I ran my hand through my hair, trying to think. How could a perfectly obnoxious little kid turn into a beetle?

"Krista!" the beetle bug screamed, "I'm going to fall. I'm at the end of a huge cliff. How did we get a cliff in our house! I'm scared!"

The beetle had crawled to the end of the seat of the chair and was just about to tumble off. I swallowed hard and reached a finger out to push the beetle back on the seat.

"Krista," the voice was desperate now. "Please

35

just turn me back into myself, and I won't ever bother you again! You can watch whatever TV programs you want whenever you want. I won't bite myself ever again and tell Mom you did it! I won't give Jason your underwear, and I won't even steal your diary anymore!"

"You stole my diary?" I couldn't believe it. "Don't I have any privacy around here at all?"

"I'm sorry!" the voice said. "Really, I am! I couldn't read it anyway because you wrote in cursive."

"What I wrote doesn't matter. It's that you took my diary, and I — " I stopped myself in mid-sentence. I was having this conversation with a black beetle bug, not a blue-eyed, blond-headed brother. Its little legs were not going to steal diaries or turn on televisions or anything else. This was nuts!

"Krista," the voice was pleading. "Turn me back, now, okay? I won't even tell Mom you did anything!"

"Tyler, I did not turn you into a beetle. You must have done something to yourself." I was sure that was true, but what if somehow it had been something I had done? What if I was responsible for this?

Just then the phone rang. I looked up to see Mrs. Pickle-Nickle answering it. I'd almost forgotten she was there. "Yes, ma'am. I made choc-

36

olate chip cookies for the children, and I'm trying to do everything I can to make them happy." She hesitated for a moment. Then she put her hand over the phone. "Your mother wants to talk to you and your brother."

I walked very slowly to the phone. I mean, what was I supposed to say, "Hi, Mom, I'm fine, but Tyler is a little black beetle bug who is about to kill himself by falling off one of the kitchen chairs. I'm sure I didn't do anything to get him that way, but no, I don't quite understand how it happened or what to do about it?"

I had a feeling that such a confession would not go over well. My mom would be hysterical, and somehow, the whole mess would end up to be my fault because I was the oldest, and I should have taken better care of Tyler. I took a deep breath. Maybe, this whole beetle thing would be over in a few minutes and Tyler would get back to normal. Besides, what could Mom do from Wichita?

I decided not to say anything. I picked up the receiver, listened to my mom, and replied, "Yes, we're fine, and we're glad you got there okay. We miss you, too. The baby-sitter is fine." Then Mom asked to talk to Tyler for a minute.

"Tyler?" I said. "You want to talk to Tyler?"

Mom's voice took on a note of concern. "Is that a problem?"

"Uhh, no," I replied, "but uhh, he's kind of busy right now."

"Krista," my mother's voice sounded stern. "Now you know he'll be upset if he finds out I called and didn't speak to him. Don't play games. Go get your brother."

"Okay," I replied. Only I wondered exactly where I should put a beetle bug to talk on the telephone. I put the phone down and walked over to the chair.

"Tyler," I whispered, "Mom's on the phone, and she wants to talk to you. If she finds out you're a beetle bug, she's going to ground us both forever, and she can't get you back to yourself while she is in Wichita anyway, so don't tell her."

"I miss Mommy!" the beetle said.

So did I, I thought. I told Tyler that I was going to carry the chair over to the phone, put the receiver on the seat, and he could crawl up onto the mouthpiece. I carried the chair real slowly so that Tyler wouldn't fall off of it, and part of me kept thinking that this must just be some weird nightmare. If so, I sure wished that I would wake up!

I put the chair down, and placed the ivory receiver face up on it. "Okay, Tyler," I whispered. "Crawl up on the mouth part."

The beetle bug began to crawl its way across the chair. It started to crawl up the receiver, and then it slipped back down the seat of the chair.

"Come on, Tyler," I hissed. "This is no time to play games."

"It's too slippery; I can't do it," the small Tyler voice whined. "Pick me up."

My mother's voice came through the receiver, "Hello? Hello? Krista, are you getting your brother? What's taking so long?"

I looked down at the little black beetle bug. It made me sick to even think of picking up a bug. I had to force my unwilling hand out to get it. "Ouch!" Tyler said. "Don't squish me!"

I put Tyler on my fingertip, and put my fingertip on the phone. He crawled off onto the mouthpiece. Then I gently put my ear to the listening part of the receiver while trying to hold the phone so Tyler wouldn't fall off. As Mom talked, I would whisper what she said, and Tyler would answer. Finally, she asked to speak to me again. "Krista, your brother just doesn't sound right to me. He sounds scared and far away. I think he must be worried that I'm not there. Now, I know he can bother you, but I want you to be especially nice to him while I'm gone. You're the oldest, and I'm counting on you." She talked to me for a minute more, and then asked to speak with the baby-sitter again, but before I gave Mrs. Pickle-Nickle the phone, Mom said, "Remember, I love you, and I trust you that no matter how much Tyler bugs you this week, you will take care of him."

I tried not to gasp at Mom's words. She couldn't have known what she was saying. I gritted my teeth, picked Tyler up from the chair, walked over to the kitchen table, and put him down gently. After peering carefully to make sure there were no other bugs on the empty chair nearest me, I sat down and put my head in my hands. I heard Mrs. Pickle-Nickle tell my mom things were okay, and then I heard her hang up the phone. How could all this have happened? In spite of the fact that I knew I had to be brave, in spite of the fact that I knew I had to keep thinking, I couldn't help it. I started to cry. When Tyler heard me crying, he started to cry again also.

"Tyler," I said through my tears, "we've just got to think of how this happened to you."

Suddenly, a voice from the other side of the room slowly said, "I think I can answer that." Mrs. Pickle-Nickle was wringing her hands, and she looked as if she were about to cry herself.

"You can?" I said in amazement. "Did you do this to Tyler?"

Mrs. Pickle-Nickle's round cheeks flushed real red. "I'm afraid I did. I'm terribly sorry. I only did it because I thought it was what you both wanted."

My mouth dropped open. "You thought we wanted you to turn him into a bug? Why would we want him to be a bug?"

Mrs. Pickle-Nickle tapped her black-booted foot nervously. "Well, you said you really wished that Tyler was a little beetle bug, and I asked you if you meant it, and you said that you definitely, absolutely did. Then Tyler said he would rather be a beetle bug, and I asked if that was what he really wished, and he said he would rather be a bug than your brother, so I thought I would make you both very happy by granting your wish. But I don't understand. Instead of being happy, all you have both done is cry, and now I feel like a failure as a baby-sitter. Really, I just wanted to make you both very happy. That's the only reason I turned Tyler into a beetle."

I repeated the words to myself to see if I had heard them right. "*You* turned Tyler into a bug because you thought it would make us happy?" Then I shook my head. "This makes no sense at all. People cannot turn other people into animals or bugs — " I stopped myself. It didn't matter if it made no sense. I wasn't seeing things. My little brother was right in front of me, and he was a beetle. What mattered most was getting Tyler back to normal. "Listen Mrs. Pickle-Nickle, if you did turn Tyler into this beetle, he doesn't want to be one, and *I* don't want him to be one, so turn him back into a person! . . . No . . . wait!" I decided I'd better not take any chances of her getting it wrong. "Turn Tyler back into my seven-year-old brother. Make him look just the way he looked before he turned into a beetle." As if to help her memory, I added, "You know, Tyler . . . he was wearing a red T-shirt and jeans. He has real blond hair and blue eyes. All you have to do to make us both real, real happy is put Tyler back just the way he was."

I held my breath. I think I was waiting to see some "Ala-Kazaam" thing from a Disney movie as Tyler turned from beetle to boy, but nothing happened. "Hey," I said, "didn't you hear me? Turn my brother back right now!"

Mrs. Pickle-Nickle sat down in the chair next to mine. "Krista, Tyler, I'm so very sorry, I really am, but I can't do that." Mrs. Pickle-Nickle bit her lip. "Are you certain that you couldn't just be happy being a beetle bug, Tyler? You seemed to like the idea so well just a little while ago. You could see and explore all kinds of places that you could never have gone as a little boy.

"And Krista, Tyler wouldn't get into your things or give Jason anything that belonged to you." She sounded so hopeful. "Maybe, it would actually be better to have a brother who was a beetle."

Tyler started to sniffle, or at least I think that's what that tiny sound was. "I don't wanna be a beetle anymore."

"Mrs. Pickle-Nickle," I said, standing up to my

full 4 feet 10 inches and trying to sound my most grown-up, "I am quite sure that it is not a good idea for Tyler to be a bug. He doesn't want to be one. I don't want him to be a bug. Now, why can't you just change him back to a person?" I was trying not to beg, but I really wanted Tyler back — just the way he was.

Mrs. Pickle-Nickle took her glasses off and began to wipe her teary eyes, which had begun to look more yellow than hazel. "Oh, you don't understand; you don't understand at all. I would if I could, but I absolutely cannot change Tyler back into a person, and that's just the start of my troubles. How could everything have gone so wrong when I tried my very hardest to make everything perfect?" And with that, Mrs. Pickle-Nickle put her elbows on the table, put her head in her hands, and began to cry.

6

It didn't seem like things could get much worse. Tyler was crawling around the center of the kitchen table. Mrs. Pickle-Nickle was crying. I was trying not to scream at our strange, weirdo baby-sitter or my bug of a brother. I took a deep breath and looked at Mrs. Pickle-Nickle. I didn't care that she said it couldn't be done. Since she had turned Tyler into a bug, she had to find a way to debug him.

I took a deep breath. Nothing I had ever learned in school was going to be any help at all in talking to Mrs. Pickle-Nickle. "So, uh, Mrs. Pickle-Nickle, do you usually turn the kids you baby-sit into bugs and stuff?"

Mrs. Pickle-Nickle sniffed. "Oh, heavens, no. I've never done it before."

I wasn't sure whether that was good or bad. At least it meant that there weren't a lot of bugs scooting around who used to be kids.

"So, uh," I continued, "how'd you do it?"

Wiping her hands on her paisley apron, Mrs. Pickle-Nickle said, "Well, I went to the Nanny Agency, and I took their training course on how to be a baby-sitter. I listened to every word. I studied my notes at night, and I memorized every word in this little book." With that she pulled a small black book from her apron pocket. I read the words on the front, which said: *The Official Nanny Agency Guide to Good Baby-sitting*.

Mrs. Pickle-Nickle held the book out to me proudly. "You can ask me anything from that book. Go ahead. I'll know it."

"Uh . . . did that book teach you to turn children into bugs?"

Mrs. Pickle-Nickle tapped her black boot on the floor. "Oh, dear. Oh, no. I don't seem to be able to explain this to you any better than I am able to baby-sit you. Let me start from the beginning." Then she stopped. "Are you sure you want to hear this? I don't want to upset you."

Upset me, I thought. Was she kidding? How could I be any more upset than I already was? I looked Mrs. Pickle-Nickle right in the eye. "Please, just tell me."

Sighing deeply, Mrs. Pickle-Nickle turned and pointed to the window. By now, it was dark out, and there wasn't much to see except some stars in the sky. "Many on my planet have had wonderful and exciting adventures, but not me. Many on my planet were selected to participate in some great study of the universe, but not me. I applied for lots of different things, but for some reason, I was never the one selected. It was upsetting, so to pass the time, I began watching more and more on my laser screen. Of all the planets, I saw on it, I enjoyed watching Earth the most. Every day, I would watch the laser screen about Earth, and then one day, it hit me; I had finally found the perfect adventure. I wrote down all the reasons why I should be allowed to do it, and then, I put on my best Talfolgom, and I went to the Zxieocm."

"Huh? you put on what and went where?"

Mrs. Pickle-Nickle twisted her hands together. "My Talfolgom, it's . . . it's . . . well, there's nothing like it on Earth. It's a special kind of coating that makes others want to hear your words, and the Zxieocm. Well, I can't believe you've never heard of that. A smart girl like you. That's the central spot of our government. It's where every really important decision is made. Well, that's why I went there. They were the only ones who could approve my adventure."

"Adventure?" I asked, still not sure I was following any of this, but willing to listen if even the slightest bit of information could get Tyler back again.

"Yes," Mrs. Pickle-Nickle's eyes glistened. "It was a grand idea. I would come to Earth and be a nanny. I would live among Earth children, and I would get to have all the fun they had. When I got back to my planet, I would be an expert on the care of Earth children. I would be most important."

Mrs. Pickle-Nickle put her hands on her ample hips. "I'll tell you. It took a long time for them to approve me, but finally the word came from the Zxieocm. I was told that I could be an Earth-children's baby-sitter. I was so excited. Don't ask! I was finally going to get to do something truly extraordinary. But the Zxieocm made it clear that before I could be a baby-sitter, I would first have to pass a training course on Earth because the first rule of the Zxieocm is that we are not to do any harm."

I looked at Tyler and wondered if turning a child into a bug was considered doing no harm. Mrs. Pickle-Nickle went on with her story, almost as if she had forgotten Tyler was there at all. Her eyes glowed that sort of yellowy color again. "Oh, I was so excited. I could hardly wait. I went home and I read everything I could find about baby-sitters. I had to design what I would look like, what my name would be."

"What you would look like?" I said, feeling a whole lot like Alice in Wonderland.

"Why yes, you don't think I could come looking the way I did. No, that would probably scare the children. So I designed myself with a dimpled smile, rosy cheeks, nice white hair, and a big soft lap."

"Uh-huh," I said, thinking that it was no wonder she looked like Mrs. Santa Claus. She had planned it.

"Then I read lots of books about baby-sitters. I liked Mary Poppins, but my favorite was a character named Mrs. Piggle-Wiggle. That's why I chose a name like hers. Anyway, then I came to Earth. It wasn't an easy trip. That UFO traffic in the universe is tough. As soon as I arrived, I immediately signed up for the Nanny Agency course because I had heard the baby-sitters from there were in high demand. I had just finished my course with an A-plus the day your mother called for a baby-sitter. So you see," she sighed deeply, "you are my very first baby-sitting job."

"Hey," called a small voice from the table, "did everyone forget about me?"

"Tyler . . . I'm trying to help. Just wait!" I said. "Go ahead, Mrs. Pickle-Nickle . . . so you came to our house to baby-sit."

She adjusted her granny glasses, which I had a feeling weren't for poor eyesight. She probably only wore them for effect. "Well, I was very nervous. I really wanted you to like me. I wanted your mother to say I was a very good baby-sitter, and right there, on page one of the *The Official Nanny Agency Guide* it says in big letters: 'A WELL BABY-SAT CHILD IS A HAPPY CHILD. TRY TO GRANT YOUR CHARGES' WISHES WHENEVER POSSIBLE.' "

Mrs. Pickle-Nickle crossed her short, chubby legs. "So I tried very hard to make you happy. I had chocolate chip cookies waiting for you. I told you, you didn't have to eat brussels sprouts, and when you both wished that Tyler was a beetle, I used my special planetary powers to turn Tyler into a bug." She sighed again. "But no one is happy. In fact, all you've both done is cry."

"It's okay," I said. I was trying to stay calm; but my heart was pounding — hard. "Listen, Mrs. Pickle-Nickle. I'll just wish very hard that Tyler was a boy again, and so will he. Then you can grant our wish. . . . You can still make us very happy. You can still be a good baby-sitter."

Mrs. Pickle-Nickle stood up and began pacing back and forth in short steps. "No, no, it won't work. You see I didn't finish explaining. I promised not to use my planetary powers here, and I just got caught up and forgot. I specifically promised not to make any major changes. See, there's no way to undo them once they're done. Once you've made a wish, you can't *un*wish it. That's what you're trying to do, and it won't work. It never does."

My voice just kind of croaked, "You mean there is no way to get Tyler back to being a human being?"

Mrs. Pickle-Nickle, or whoever or whatever she really was, continued pacing back and forth. "Well, the good news is that eventually, the power wears off — "

"Oh good," I interrupted. "Then we just have to wait a little while and Tyler will be back to being Tyler."

"I don't think it's that simple. It could be a very long time." Mrs. Pickle-Nickle frowned. "To tell you the truth, I really don't know how Earth time and Zxieocm powers work together." She sighed. "I don't suppose your mother would be very pleased to return and find that her son was a beetle, would she?"

The look on my face must have been enough of an answer. "Drat! I wish I had thought of all that before I turned him into a beetle. You're not happy, your brother isn't happy, and I don't suppose your mother will give me any kind of a recommendation at all. I've really made a terrible fiasco of my Earth experience. I fear that dealing with Earth children is a lot more complicated than I thought it could possibly be. I just didn't understand that Earth children bicker and say harsh things to each other that they really don't mean."

Mrs. Pickle-Nickle was still pacing. Her little black boots made clicking noises against the tile on the kitchen floor. It was almost as if she was talking to herself now. "As I see it, there's only one thing left for me to do."

"Oh, good," I broke in, "then you still have an idea."

"Yes," she said, "I'm going home before I destroy anything else. I don't like it on Earth after all. I just shouldn't have come, but it was nice meeting you."

"You can't go home now! You can't leave two kids by themselves, especially when one of them isn't even a kid anymore."

Mrs. Pickle-Nickle folded her pudgy arms across her chest. "Yes, I can go home, and that is *exactly* what I am going to do." She put one hand inside her apron pocket, and her eyes began to glow yellow. They got brighter and brighter and brighter. The whole room took on a yellow glow, and pretty soon, Mrs. Pickle-Nickle was so

51

covered in a bright yellow light that I couldn't even look at her. "Good-bye and good luck," she called.

Then there was silence. All of a sudden, the golden glow faded, and I looked around. The room was completely empty except for me and a little black beetle on the kitchen table.

7

"**M**rs. Pickle-Nickle," I called. "Mrs. Pickle-Nickle, wherever you're hiding, please come out? You can't just leave us alone." I crossed my fingers and hoped to hear the sound of her clicking little black boots, but there was only silence.

"Is she really gone?" came the beetle's scratchy voice. "Who's going to take care of us? I'm scared, and I'm hungry, and I don't want to be a beetle anymore!" The voice grew softer, "Krista, she's gone, huh? What are we gonna do?"

I took a deep breath. We were going to do the only thing we could, the only thing that made sense — call Mom and let her figure out what to do. I walked over to the phone, picked it up, and then stopped suddenly. How was I going to explain this mess to my mother? I cleared my throat and practiced into the dial tone. "Hi, Mom. Yes, I know we talked to you a little while ago, and I said that everything was fine, but I lied." I stopped for a minute and thought about it. No, that wasn't the way to say it; I always got in trouble for lying.

I tried again. "Hi, Mom. It's me, Krista, and I'm fine, really I am. But the baby-sitter turned out to be an alien who went back to her own planet, and before she left, she turned Tyler into a beetle bug. Do you think you could come home now?" I thought about how that sounded. Even though it was the truth, it sounded so awful that Mom would probably think I was lying — or she'd just faint. Maybe, I shouldn't tell her everything, especially the part about Tyler.

I tried once more. "Hi, Mom? Don't worry, but the baby-sitter had to go home. Tyler isn't exactly himself, and I don't know how to take care of him. Could you please come back because we really need you." There, I thought, that was the truth, mostly, and it wasn't so scary that Mom would faint or think I was lying.

"Hey," came Tyler's voice. "What are you doing? Why do you just keep telling Mom the story? What is she saying?"

I pulled at the threads on the end of my blue sweater sleeve. "Tyler, I haven't even called yet. I'm just practicing to try to get the words right."

"Well, hurry up!" the voice squeaked. "I miss Mommy, and I want her, and if you don't call right now, I'm going to."

I looked at the small black beetle. "Yeah, right. Are you going to use your antennae or one of your little legs to call?"

Tyler started to cry, and I felt really bad. I shouldn't have said that; I really shouldn't have. It was just that I wasn't exactly sure what I was doing, and I didn't need Tyler to complain about what I was trying to do. I looked at the phone number my mother had posted on the wall and began to dial. My hand was shaking. "Oh, please," I said a little prayer to myself as the phone rang, "don't let Mom end up blaming me for this and grounding me for the rest of my life."

"Wichita Country Inn," said a voice at the other end of the line.

"Uh, yes, uh, I'd like to talk to my mom."

"Hmmm," said the voice with a chuckle, "I imagine we have a lot of moms here. Who would yours be?"

"Mrs. Barbara Klausner," I said biting my lip. Already I was messing things up, and Mom hadn't even come to the phone yet.

"Just a moment, I'll ring her room." The phone rang, and my stomach sank to the floor. If only I could get all the words out straight, and if only she could still get home tonight, maybe everything would be okay.

The phone rang and rang, and no one answered. Finally, there was a woman's voice on the other end. "Mom!" I almost shouted. "I'm so glad you're there."

"I'm so sorry," the woman's voice said, and I knew it wasn't my mom. "There's no answer in her room."

"But . . ." I said trying to fight back the tears, "I really, really need to talk to her."

"Well," said the hotel woman's voice, "let me check her box for messages. Maybe, she's left word." There was silence on the phone, and when the hotel woman came back, she said, "I'm so sorry, but your mother has left a note for her boss that says the client wanted her to visit a supplier and was driving her there. She'll be staying in a private home near the supplier and will call her boss when she knows more." The hotel woman's voice sounded concerned, "Is an adult there with you? Perhaps, I should speak to an adult."

"It's okay," I said feeling a million years old. There was nothing this hotel lady could do to help, and Mom couldn't be reached. "We just wanted to tell Mom we miss her a lot." I hung up the phone and crossed my arms in front of me. We were truly home alone. It was what I had always dreamed about, but not like this. My brother was a beetle, and I was in charge of taking care of us both. Even in my favorite, warmest blue sweater, I felt cold.

"Hey," came Tyler's voice, "did you talk to Mom? Is she coming home?"

I looked over to the kitchen table, and I saw the small black beetle bug at the table's very edge. "Tyler," I screamed, "don't move. You're about to fall off." I ran back to the light-oak table, and trying not to squirm at touching a bug, I pushed Tyler back more to the center. "What were you doing?" I yelled. "You just about got yourself killed!"

The bug almost seemed to be shaking. Its antennae were waving wildly. "I didn't know I was so close. You can't imagine what our table looks like from here. I can't see so good anymore, and I'm not sure how I'm supposed to use these things on the top of my head."

I ran my hand through my hair. I had no idea how a beetle was supposed to act, but I couldn't have my little brother killing himself. I told Tyler not to move at all, and that I would be right back. Then I ran upstairs to my room and got the box that my tennis shoes had come in. Running back down again, I yelled, "Tyler, you better not have moved." When I got back, he was in the exact same spot. I put the box down in front of him. "Okay," I encouraged, "now all you have to do is just crawl in this box. That way, you can't accidentally fall off something."

"I don't want be in a box," Tyler whined.

"You don't want to be dead!" I commanded. "Now get in."

Tyler didn't argue anymore; in fact, he really tried to climb in, but the box was like a wall a million miles high to him. Finally, after I turned the box on its side, Tyler crawled down into it. Then I set the box upright again and breathed a big sigh of relief. At least, he wasn't going to get killed in the next few minutes.

"Krista, I'm hungry," the beetle said, and I looked at the clock. It was almost seven-thirty, much later than our normal dinnertime. Of course, nothing was normal anymore, and Tyler was hungry. I had no idea what a beetle ate, but I also couldn't let Tyler starve to death. "I'll go outside and get you some grass," I said. It was dark out, and I wasn't thrilled by the idea, but I was the older sister. And right now, I was all Tyler had.

"Grass?" came the little voice. "Yuck! Why would I want grass? I want chocolate ice cream!"

"Tyler," I replied, "I don't know much about beetles, but I'm almost sure that none of them eat chocolate ice cream, and besides, Mom would be really mad if she found out that's what we had for dinner."

"Krista," said the little voice, "it's been awful enough to be turned into a beetle; I ought to at least get what I want for dinner. And I don't care what other beetles eat. Other beetles didn't used to be boys."

Actually, chocolate ice cream sounded pretty good to me, too. Besides, for once, Tyler was right; we had both been through a lot. If we had to be home alone like this, there might as well be something good about it. I got out the container of ice cream from the freezer. I put a little piece of tin foil down on the bottom of Tyler's box, and I spooned a little bit of chocolate ice cream onto the foil. Tyler crawled over to the ice cream. Even though I had put less than a teaspoon in the box, the ice-cream mound was bigger than Tyler. Still, it didn't seem to be bothering him, and as I watched, the ice cream began to disappear. Satisfied that he wouldn't starve, I got out a big bowl and a spoon for myself. I put two scoops in the bowl, which was the most my mother ever let me have at one time; then I looked at the ice cream, thought about my day, and added two more big scoops.

After eating four scoops of ice cream with chocolate sauce and whipped cream, the world didn't look quite so terrible. Maybe Tyler would turn back into himself by tomorrow. Maybe Mom would come home and find out that I really was very grown-up and could handle anything.

The ice cream must have made Tyler feel better, too, because he said, "I can't wait to go to school tomorrow; I'm going to crawl right onto Jennifer Patrick's desk. She thinks she's so neat *and* she hates bugs." There was a tiny chuckle from the shoe box. "Just wait till she sees me. Maybe I'll even crawl right into her hair. You'll probably be able to hear her scream all the way to your class. Boy, I can't wait!"

I didn't say anything to Tyler, but there was no way he could go to school tomorrow. I mean, he'd probably never live through the day. I remembered one day right after school started this fall, Jason had captured a fly. The boys had dared him to eat the fly, and so Jason had put it in his mouth, and swallowed it. I shuddered. It was disgusting, but typical Jason. I couldn't take a chance on something like that happening to Tyler. He'd just have to stay home from school, which brought up another big problem. Just how was he going to get excused?

My red backpack was still lying on the kitchen floor right next to Tyler's blue one where we had dropped them when we had first come into the kitchen for cookies that afternoon. That seemed like a very long time ago. I walked over to the backpack and pulled out my notebook. In the tiniest letters at the very bottom, I had written *I like J.L.* No one would ever see them except me, but it made me feel like I had a special secret. I took out a piece of notebook paper, and I began to write: *Please excuse Tyler Klausner. He is sick, and he may be —* I wanted to write *contagious*, but I had no idea how to spell it, so I tore up the paper and began again. *Please excuse Tyler Klausner. He is sick and will come to school when he is feeling better.* I signed it *Mrs. Pickle-Nickle, the baby-sitter.* Then I examined what I had written. The writing looked like a kid's. The note would never work.

Walking over to the desk drawer, I took a piece of Mom's best blue stationery. Real carefully, I scrunched my letters together more, and I wrote *Please excuse Tyler Klausner. He has a bug and will return when he feels more like himself. Mrs. Pickle-Nickle, baby-sitter.*

I held the note up. It looked like a grown-up could have written it! The stationery was a nice touch. I read it again. Except for the signature, the note was almost the truth.

"What're you doing?" came Tyler's tiny voice. "I can't see anything in here except a gray box."

Tonight there was no point in arguing with Tyler about not going to school. It could wait until tomorrow, so I said, "Uh . . . I was just doing some homework."

"Yow!" called the beetle. "I have to memorize my spelling words for tomorrow. How can I do that?"

"Aw, don't worry about it, Tyler."

"Really? Boy, maybe, it's not so bad to have you in charge. Mom would definitely make me study my spelling list."

"Yeah," I joked, "I keep telling you you're lucky to have me for your sister." But poor Tyler wasn't very lucky; somehow, he still thought his life was going to go on just the way it had before he had become a beetle. I started picking at my sweater sleeve again. It was a terrible habit I had whenever I got nervous, and I had ruined a couple of sweaters that way. I decided that right now there was no point to having Tyler face the fact that he might have to live out his life in a box, so I said, "It's late. I'm gonna put my stuff away. Let's just go to sleep." I started to get up from the table. I guessed he'd be safe right in that box, right in the middle of the kitchen table.

"Hey," came a voice as I switched off the light. "Why did it get so dark in here? Krista, this isn't funny."

"Sorry," I said, "I'll leave on the light."

"Wait," called the beetle. "Get me out of this box! How can I go to bed if I'm in some dumb box with high walls."

I came back to the kitchen table. "Tyler," I said speaking to the box, "beetles don't sleep in beds. Besides, you might fall off the edge. You'd better stay in the box."

"Wait. Don't go. I'm scared to stay down here all by myself."

I sat down on the chair and tried to think. Finally, I said, "How about if I put your box upstairs on your bed. Then you'll be safe, and you won't be scared." Tyler seemed to like that idea pretty well, and once again, I felt very proud of myself. I was getting to be a really good problem solver. I carried the box far in front of me so that I didn't have to really look at the beetle. If I could just listen to Tyler's voice and not look at him, I could almost forget that I hated bugs as much as I hated snakes, and that my brother was now an ugly little black bug.

I walked into Tyler's room and gently put the box down on his bed. "Sleep tight, and don't let the bed bugs — " I stopped midsentence. Though Mom always said that to us when she tucked us in, tonight they didn't seem like quite the right words to use.

I hadn't even gotten halfway out of Tyler's room when I heard, "Krista, I don't think this is gonna work."

"Why not?"

"Cuz I can't tell that I'm in my bed. All I can see are these gray box walls, and I'm scared. This box is hard, not soft like my bed. If I really have to stay in this dumb box, I wanna sleep in your room. That way if I have bad dreams, you'll be right there."

I didn't have the heart to argue. So after I put on my favorite red flannel nightgown with the blue-and-gold hearts, I carried Tyler in his box into my room. I put the box down on my desk. I even put some cotton in the bottom of the box so it would be soft for Tyler. Then I climbed into my own bed. Usually, about the only thing I hated more than having Tyler in my room was having bugs in my room, and now I had both all wrapped up in one. The only good thing was that at least he couldn't fly. I often slept with my mouth open. I had allergies, and I slept better that way. Anyway, when I was younger, I used to have bad dreams about a bug flying in my mouth while I slept.

"Good night, Krista," came Tyler's scared voice. "Thanks for being such a good big sister."

"It's okay, Tyler." It was dumb, but I felt really good about what he had said. Maybe everything would work out if we just didn't panic. I lay in bed thinking about how early I would have to get up in the morning to be able to walk to school and get there on time. I considered just staying home, but I didn't want to make the teachers suspicious. Both of us home tomorrow might bring questions. All we needed were the school people poking around here. Even if Tyler did turn back into a person, neither one of us would ever live the story down. I snuggled into my covers. Maybe, the worst of this was all over. In fact, I felt almost sure that since we had done so well tonight, all we had to do was keep our secret a little longer, and Tyler would turn right back into his old self.

Suddenly, there was a shout. Heart pounding, I switched on the light quickly. "What is it? What's wrong?"

"I think I have wings tucked under here. Krista, I think I can fly!"

8

"**D**on't move!" I ordered. "And do NOT even think about flying." It wasn't bad enough that my only little brother was a repulsive-looking black beetle bug with skinny little black legs and waving antennae, but now he thought he should take to the air.

"Why can't I fly? It might even make it not so bad to have to be a beetle bug. I mean flying looks like lots of fun. Remember when Mom took us to see *Peter Pan*? You wanted to be Wendy so you could fly, too."

"That was different."

"Yeah, what was different was that then neither one of us could fly. Now I can and you can't, so you don't want me to. You never want me to have any fun!"

I got out of bed and walked very quietly over toward my closet. If I could just remember where I had put the lid to the box, everything would be okay. Tyler was wrong about my being jealous; I did not want to be a beetle bug even if it did mean that I could fly. However, I was scared to death of flying bugs, and I certainly did not plan to sleep in the same room with one. Spying the Reebok shoe lid on the floor of my closet, I moved my sneakers, pushed aside some dirty clothes, and picked up the box lid.

"Hey! I hear noises. What's going on?"

"I'll be right there, Tyler," I said, hurrying over to the box and firmly clamping the lid on the top of it.

Tyler's voice was very muffled. "What happened? Why'd it get so dark? Hey, Krista, what's going on?"

"What's going on," I said, "is that I put a lid on your box."

"Well, take it off! It's dark, and it's not fair. I'm gonna tell Mom on you."

"Look, it's only for your own good. You may be a beetle, but you don't know how to do anything a beetle does. Didn't you almost crawl off the table because you couldn't see and didn't know how to use your antennae? Didn't you eat chocolate ice cream, and what beetle does that? What if you try to fly, and you kill yourself? Then how will we ever get you back into being a boy? Besides, when I looked, you didn't even have wings."

Tyler pleaded with me to take the lid off the box. "At least look and see if I have wings. I just want to know if I do. I promise, super-duper, double-cross-my-heart promise that I won't fly away. Please, please, *please*? Besides, maybe I won't even be able to breathe very long with a lid on this box. Maybe you're killing me."

He had a point. I had no idea if a beetle could breathe in a box with a lid on it. It was true that I did not like my little brother that much, but it just didn't seem fair to kill him when he was only a bug, and I was still me. I took the lid off the box. "Remember, you promised — no flying!" I reminded him.

"Okay, now look. Do I have wings?"

I forced myself to get down close to the beetle, even though the thought of my face being that near a bug practically made me sick. Tyler was right. He did have wings. They were stiff and shiny, and were folded back. Swell. When I told him what I saw, he yelped with delight. "I'll bet I'm the only kid in my class who can fly!"

I just knew he was going to take off in spite of his promise not to. "Tyler, right now you are not a kid, and if you try to fly, you may never be a kid again. So don't do it!" I made him cross his heart, if a beetle could do such a thing, and swear that he couldn't watch any of his TV shows ever again if he tried to fly. I told him I was getting back into bed and turning out the lights because we would have a lot to do in the morning, and we had to get some sleep before then. He listened to me even though neither one of us had any idea of whether a beetle needed to sleep during the night. Soon all was quiet in my room. In the soft shadows of my Little Mermaid night-light, I could see the outline of Tyler's shoe box.

I lay in my bed, but I didn't go to sleep. For one thing, I was half expecting Tyler to start flying around the room. For another, I had no idea what I was supposed to feed him for breakfast, or how I was going to break it to him that he could not go to school in his present state. There were just so many questions to be answered. One thing was for sure, I was never letting any baby-sitter in the house again who looked like Mrs. Santa Claus and had a name like Mrs. Pickle-Nickle and made snacks like homemade chocolate chip cookies for us.

I don't remember, but I guess I must have finally gone to sleep because all of a sudden, the alarm was ringing, and it was light in my room. For a minute, I blinked, and hoped that Tyler would be a seven-year-old boy asleep in his bed. Then I saw the box on my desk. "Tyler? . . ." I questioned.

"Uh-huh, do we have to get up for school already?" replied his sleepy voice.

"Uhh, no . . . you can sleep some more. I'm just going to start getting ready." I decided that there was no point to telling him that he wasn't going to school until the absolute last minute. I looked in my closet and picked out some clothes to wear to school. At first, I took out a pair of red pants and a red-and-white sweater, but then I put them back and chose my baggy jeans and a green flannel shirt. It was kind of nice to make my own decisions about things and know that no one was going to tell me that something else might look better.

Not that I really thought Tyler could see out of the box or anything, but still, I took my clothes into the bathroom and got dressed. When I got back to my room, Tyler was calling, "This is the last time I'm yelling for you. I can't crawl out of this box, and if you don't come here, I'm going to try to fly out!"

I took a deep sigh. Bug or boy, my brother was still a pain. "I'm right here; I just went to get dressed. Now, I'm going to pick up the box, take it downstairs, and get us both some breakfast."

As I walked toward the kitchen, Tyler started talking. It was so weird to hear him; it was like his voice was his, but it was too high and squeaky to really be his. "Maybe, you'd better come into my class and drop me off at my seat today so all my friends will know it's me. And maybe you'd better tell my teacher who I am. I don't think she like bugs so well. We have a frog in the aquarium in the back of the room, and sometimes she feeds him bugs."

I decided to put off telling Tyler about not going to school a little longer. There was no point to fighting until we had to. "Let's worry about breakfast right now. What do you suppose a beetle eats for breakfast?"

"I dunno," Tyler replied, "but I want French toast."

"No way, Tyler!"

"Oh, now I suppose you're going to tell me that beetles can't eat French toast. Well, maybe normal ones can't, but that's what I feel like eating."

Through gritted teeth, I said, "I am not making French toast because it's hard to make, and just in case you forgot, we don't have any grown-ups here to do it for us. So unless you can crawl out of that box and make it for us . . ." I walked over to the freezer and pulled out some Eggo waffles. "We're both having waffles, and they'll just have to do!"

"Geez," came the scratchy voice in the box, "you don't have to have a cow over it."

I put two waffles in the toaster and waited for them to pop up. When they did, I put mine on my plate, cut the other waffle in half, and plunked it in the box.

Suddenly, a scream came from the box. "Yiikkes! Help!" I peered in, but all I could see was the waffle, no Tyler.

"Hey, where are you?" My heart started to pound.

"I'm under here. Are you trying to kill me?"

Carefully, I picked up the waffle. I'd put it down on top of Tyler. The good news was that it had landed so that Tyler was safe in one of the indentations. The bad news was that he was very scared. I told Tyler I was really, really sorry and took the waffle out of the box. I cut off a tiny piece, squashed it into even smaller pieces, and carefully laid it in the box. I took a small plastic milk lid, put water in it, and laid it carefully, in the box. Finally, Tyler calmed down and began to eat, and so did I.

As I ate, I thought that if the whole thing hadn't been so crazy, it would have almost been funny. "Girl Kills Brother With Half a Waffle." It was like something out of the newspapers Mom read in the supermarket lines.

Breakfast was over, and I cleared my plate even though no one was there to see me do it or care if it was done. I was stalling, and I knew it. It was time for me to leave for school. Carefully, I read the note I'd written last night excusing Tyler from school. It still looked pretty grown-up. I slipped it into my backpack. I knew that Tyler would insist on going to school if he thought I wanted him to stay home, so I thought and thought, and then I had it. "Hey, Tyler," I said, "*Star Trek* is on this morning, and since you've had to go through so much in being a bug and stuff, I won't tell on you if you want to stay home and watch TV."

"Wow! You won't — and there aren't even any grown-ups to make me go either. How neat! Take me into the family room and let's turn on the TV right now."

This was great; it was going to be even easier than I thought it could possibly be. Tyler would stay here safely until I could get home from school, and then if he still hadn't turned back into a person, we would figure out what to do next.

I took Tyler's box into the family room and turned on the television. "I can't see anything but this gray box! This is no fun at all! I'm not staying in this thing anymore. I'm gonna fly out of here right now."

"Tyler!" I warned sternly. "You promised no flying!" I scrunched up my face and half closed my eyes so I wouldn't have to really look at the bug, and then I reached my finger down into the box.

"Come on, I'll put you on the coffee table right in front of the TV."

I put Tyler on the coffee table. I filled the plastic lid with more water and put it next to him, and then I told him that I was going to get my backpack and go to school. Before I even made it out of the room, Tyler called, "Wait. Krista, my eyes don't work right or something, but I can't see the TV very well, and I don't want to be here all by myself all day. I'm gonna come to school with you after all."

Coming back into the family room, I sat down on the sofa. "Tyler, listen to me. You *can't* go to school. First of all, it would be much too easy for someone to accidentally squash you. Even if everyone was real careful, Tyler; think about it. I mean, Mrs. Pickle-Nickle said the spell would wear off, but what will happen when it does? You'll never live down having been a bug. Everyone will tease you for the rest of your life. Kids'll say stuff like, 'There's a roach, get the RAID!' or 'Boy, I don't know why, but Tyler always bugs me.' It'll be awful." I knew I was right, and not only would the kids tease Tyler, but as his sister, I'd get my share, too. Especially from certain people like Jason, who could always find things to tease people about.

Tyler started to cry. "I don't think I like being

a bug anymore. I don't want to get squished. I don't want to get teased for my whole life, and I DO NOT want to stay here in this house all by myself all day. Mommy never lets me stay home alone, and now that I'm a bug, I can't even call 9-1-1 if I need help."

I looked at the clock. If I didn't leave pretty soon, I was going to be late, and I especially didn't want anyone to notice me today. I ran my hand, through my hair, twisting one of my curls as I thought. In a way, Tyler was right. It could be really dangerous for him to stay home alone. But I was right, too. He just couldn't go to school today. I didn't know what to do. At ten and a half, I just didn't think I was smart enough to figure this one out. But I had to. I mean, who could I call for advice?

Then a small, scratchy voice piped up. "If I can't go to my own class, then I'll just come to yours with you."

"With me . . . you'll come to my class? I don't think so. . . ."

"Please, Krista, you just can't leave me here all alone all day. I wouldn't do that to you. How would you have liked it if Mrs. Pickle-Nickle had turned you into a beetle?"

I gulped at the thought of that, and then I decided that maybe, just maybe, Tyler could come to school with me. I could put him in a smaller box than the shoe box he was in now, and then when I got to school, I could put the box inside my desk. No one would even have to know what was in the box. That way Tyler would be safe with me, but no one else would know he was at school.

It wasn't perfect, but at least it was a plan. It would have to work, and then, if Tyler hadn't turned back into himself by nighttime, I would get hold of Mom in Wichita. I told Tyler that he could come to school with me, and then I ran upstairs looking for the bracelet box that I'd gotten for my birthday. Pulling it out of my top drawer, I stared at it longingly for just a minute. My pretty satin-lined box that I had planned to save forever just wasn't going to be the same after having had a beetle live in it. But I couldn't worry about that now; I ran downstairs to put Tyler in the box. Still not too thrilled about picking up beetles, I put both boxes on their sides and let Tyler crawl out of one and into the other. As the little black bug made his way into my bracelet box, I thought of all the times that I had screamed at Tyler that I didn't want him touching my stuff because he had cooties. Now it was probably true! My bracelet box would be ruined. If I didn't know how miserable he was as a beetle, I would almost think he had done this whole thing on purpose, just to creep me out.

"Tyler, I'm going to have to put the lid on this box until we get to school."

"No! No! Don't!"

"I'll poke holes in it in case you need them to breathe, but everyone would think it was just too weird if I came in carrying a beetle. I mean everyone knows that I don't like bugs and snakes. It just wouldn't work to have to start answering all kinds of questions." Tyler protested again, but this time I wasn't giving in. The lid was going on the box, or Tyler wasn't coming to school with me.

At first he threatened just to fly away forever so he didn't have to have me boss him around anymore. I told him to go ahead. He'd probably get eaten by a cat. In the end, he gave in, and sadly, I punched holes in the lid of my favorite box. Pulling on my pink windbreaker and hoisting my backpack over my left shoulder, I picked up the bracelet box, and I began the walk to school. Although we always walked home, Mom took us to school in the morning, and I hoped with all the delays, that I had still left early enough not to be tardy. Today, of all days, I did not want to make a big entrance.

When I got out the door, I saw Jason leaving

his house, and I hurried even faster so he couldn't possibly catch up to me. I did not need his questions about my box, especially since the box was talking nonstop. "Krista, tell me where we are right now. Krista, don't jiggle me so much; I'll throw up. Krista, what are you gonna tell my teacher? Hey, Krista, are there any good rocks to kick to school?"

Finally, we got to the playground gate. "Tyler," I hissed, because I didn't want anyone to see me talking to myself. "We're at school. You've got to be quiet now."

"But . . . you mean I can't talk to you all day long? It's no fair if you get to be the one talking."

Oh boy, I thought to myself, having a brother as a beetle was not easy. "I'm not going to talk to you either. If I did, people would think I was talking to myself. I promise that if you just be quiet, I'll . . . I'll answer every one of your questions about the whole day, and I won't even get mad or anything! But if you talk, I'll . . . well . . . I'll dump you out the window, and you'll be on your own forever and ever or until you get eaten up."

I know it was a terrible thing to say, and I felt bad about saying it, but I didn't have any more time to talk to Tyler. School was almost starting, and I couldn't have a talking box. I'd make it up to Tyler tonight. I'd give him some extra chocolate ice cream.

The warning tardy bell rang, and I took a deep breath. Carrying the box in my left hand, I walked in through the gates, pushed open the door of the school building and headed for room 5-A.

9

Walking down the hall, I looked neither left nor right, hoping that if I didn't say hi to anyone, no one would say hi to me or ask me why I was carrying a bracelet box so carefully. Luck must have been with me because I was able to slide into my seat and gently put the box in my desk without anyone seeming to notice. Tyler and I had made a deal that I would take the lid off the box once I got it safely in my desk, and as I bent down to do so, I whispered, "Now, remember, absolutely no talking today!"

The bell rang, and the P.A. came on as it did every day. "Good morning, boys and girls. Please rise for the Pledge of Allegiance." I adjusted Tyler's box, stood, and began to recite, "I pledge allegiance . . ." and a small squeaky voice coming from my desk joined in with the class.

Horrified, I was sure that the people around me must be hearing the added voice. This called for drastic and immediate action. I pretended to drop a pencil and bent down to get it. "Tyler," I whispered as I bent down toward my desk, "shut up!"

The pledge finished, and everyone took their seats. Mrs. Kendall frowned at me as she said, "Class, let us remember that we all recite the pledge standing and looking at the flag. Even if we've dropped a pen or pencil, we wait until after the pledge to pick it up." Several kids in the class turned to look at me, and Jason grinned and shook his head at me. Mrs. Kendall continued, "Now, please take your math books from your desks, and let's turn our attention to multiplying fractions."

I sighed. This day was going to be even worse than I had worried about it being. For the first few minutes of math, I didn't even hear Mrs. Kendall's explanations. With bated breath, I kept waiting for Tyler to pipe up with something he just thought he had to say. How could I concentrate on simple equations when I knew how quiet the room was and that if Tyler said anything there was no doubt that all the kids around my desk would hear him? But the minutes passed silently. Tyler surprised me. He was very good during math. He didn't even say anything when I accidentally moved his box while getting a piece of paper out of my desk.

We moved into reading, and I was getting less nervous. Maybe we really would get through this day. Then Tyler would turn back into himself, and

— then a terrible thought hit me. What if Tyler turned back into himself right here in this classroom? How would I ever be able to explain my seven-year-old brother appearing from out of my desk? Try as I might, I could not think of any excuses that would explain such a thing to the class. Jason would have a field day with that. I could almost hear his voice. "Ahh, look Krista's a magician, and since she couldn't stand to be without her little brother, she brought him right here to our class."

I started looking inside my desk every minute or two just to make sure Tyler was still a beetle. Pretending to study my book, I tried to look interested in reading, but the words were swimming across the page. I glanced up, and accidentally saw Jason. When he saw I was looking at him, he started looking inside his desk and then grinned. That boy! All I needed was for him to suspect something. As much as I wanted to, I forced myself not to look down at my desk again.

"Krista," Mrs. Kendall said, "I repeat . . . would you begin reading where Jennifer left off?"

I hadn't heard her ask me the first time, and I had no idea where Jennifer was. "Mrs. Kendall, could I read that part?" It was Cindy; she was the very top of the very top reading group. Usually, she was kind of a pain, but today all I could think of was thank goodness for teachers' pets.

Fortunately, after reading, it was time for recess. Michelle came by my desk, "Meet you at our spot on the playground."

I didn't answer because I knew I couldn't go out to the playground with Michelle and Julia, and I knew that I wasn't going to explain why. The truth was that I had to go the library and see if there were any books on alien spells or beetles. Besides, Mrs. Milligan, our librarian, was practically deaf, and if no one else was in the library, I could take Tyler with me and talk to him without anyone hearing or caring. Sadly, I watched everyone else gladly head out to the playground. When they were gone, I put the lid on my bracelet box, and I carried it toward the library.

I wasn't looking forward to being in our library. Mrs. Milligan wouldn't wear her hearing aid, but she still insisted on having conversations with the kids who came in. It could take forever just to get a book. I remembered the last time I'd come in during recess. It had been in the very beginning of the year, right after social studies. Mrs. Kendall had announced that she would give a prize to the first person who could find out the name of the doctor who had tried to help Abraham Lincoln when he was shot. I figured I could run into the library at recess, find out, and win the prize. It was the first time I'd met Mrs. Milligan, our new librarian. "Could you help me find out about the doctor who helped Lincoln?" I had asked. After a few "huhs" from Mrs. Milligan, I repeated the question four times, finally yelling it at the top of my lungs.

"Yes, yes." Mrs. Milligan smiled. "Well, Lincolns are cars. Let's go look in the card catalogue to see what we have about cars."

The bell ending recess had rung before I ever learned one thing about Abraham Lincoln's doctor. Other students had similar stories to tell about dealing with our librarian, and now, everyone pretty much stayed away from the library unless a teacher was with them.

The library was completely empty when I got in, and today, I was very glad. I put Tyler's box on one of the library tables in the back of the room, and then I pulled a book off the shelf and sat down. Opening the book and hiding the box behind it, I took off the box lid. "Hey, Tyler . . . how're you doing?"

The beetle didn't move. "Tyler," I said softly but urgently. "Are you okay?" The beetle still didn't move, and my heart started pounding. What if my little brother-bug was dead? "Tyler!" I said a little louder.

"Uh-huh," the beetle said. "I guess I was sleeping." But he woke up fast and tried to make up for not talking all morning. "I hate this. I'm so bored. I can't talk, and I can't play my video

84

games, and I can't even move around. If I have to be at school, I like being in my own class better than being in yours. And I hate not having recess. Are we at home? Can I get out of this little box now?"

Tyler groaned when he found out that it was only morning recess. Then I told him that we were in the library. "Yikes! With Mrs. Milligan? How come?" he asked.

"So I can try to find out whether there's anything that's been written about aliens and beetles. Besides, the library is empty except for Mrs. Milligan, and we can talk without anyone hearing us. Now, when I get back from my lunch, I'm going to slip a potato chip into your box, and I'll save a little of my milk from my lunch and somehow, I'll find something to bring it back to you in."

"That's it . . . all I get for lunch is a potato chip and leftover milk?" And Tyler began to cry. I really did feel sorry for him. It couldn't be much fun to be a beetle bug in a box, but I was doing everything I could to take care of him, and it was his fault as much as mine that he was in this awful mess.

I spent recess in the library. The only book I could find about aliens said that they were made-up creatures and didn't really exist. Stupid book. I could certainly tell that writer about at least one alien that definitely did exist. I had better luck with information about beetles. There were a bunch of books on insects, and one whole book just on beetles. It was called *Keeping Minibeasts: Beetles*. The title was a perfect description of Tyler because he had been a minibeast even before he had been a beetle. There were lots of pictures in the book, and I found out there were lots of different kinds of beetles. I was sure Tyler wouldn't be interested in the kinds of things any of these beetles ate! Then I read about the beetle's development; it told how a beetle went from a mealworm, to a pupa, to an adult beetle. That was no help at all. My beetle had gone from boy to beetle with no stages in between.

I also found a section on beetles' life cycles, and I turned to it, biting my lip, and hoping that beetles lived long enough to allow Tyler to turn back into a boy. But the book didn't say how long beetles lived. It did say to be careful when picking a beetle up because you could permanently damage it, and that you shouldn't worry if the beetle gave off a smelly fluid in your hand. Well, at least Tyler hadn't done that yet.

The bell signaling the end of recess rang, and I took Tyler back to class. Michelle and Julia looked at me strangely, and I tried to pretend everything was okay. At lunchtime, Michelle and Julia asked me where I had been at recess, and when I said the library, Julia said, "Uh-oh, you must be mad at us. No one goes to the library during recess. So what did we do, and why didn't you just tell us about it instead of going to the library?"

"I wasn't mad, I just had some stuff I had to do."

"Like what?" Michelle asked.

"Uhh . . . I . . . uh . . . I just wanted to look at some books." I knew it sounded lame, even to me, but I wasn't ready to share my awful secret with anyone yet, not even my best friends. I just kept hoping that no one would have to know the truth.

Julia folded her arms across her chest and glared at me. "Krista, if you're mad at us, just say so, but don't be a dumb baby and lie about it. Well . . ."

I didn't need this now. I really didn't. "Can't you guys just leave me alone?" I blurted.

Julia and Michelle seemed surprised, but Michelle said, "Fine, then we won't bother you." They took their lunches and moved to a different table. I finished my lunch by myself. What a morning! I'd gotten yelled at by my teacher, missed having any fun at recess, and now my two best friends were mad at me. The only positive I could think of was that at least it would be easy for me to walk back to the room by myself and slip Tyler the potato chip. I took my milk carton and the potato chip bag and headed back to class to wait for Mrs. Kendall to come and open the door.

I was the first one in the classroom, and as everyone else filed in the room, I opened the box in my desk, put in a piece of potato chip, and poured a little of my milk into a juice cap from lunch. "Okay, Tyler," I whispered, "hang in there. Here's lunch, and it's already afternoon."

While Mrs. Kendall started putting some social studies stuff on the board, Jason got up, walked by my desk to sharpen his pencil and said, "Hey, do you always feed your desk parts of your lunch?"

My face turned bright red, but I totally ignored him. How did he always seem to know what I was doing? As Mrs. Kendall started the afternoon class, she talked about a social studies extra-credit project that we could do over the weekend if we wanted. We were to find and work with a partner to write and reenact a conversation between two people involved in World War I. She said we could have five minutes to talk among ourselves about it. Jeff, who only sat two seats from me, seemed as if he was leaning toward my desk. I thought he was even going to talk to me. I hoped my hair still looked curly instead of frizzy. I'd had so much to worry about today that I had barely even thought about Jeff until that minute. "Krista, do you want to be partners? I'm going out of town with my family tomorrow, but we could work tonight."

Did I want to be partners? Was he kidding? It was like a dream. Every girl in the fifth grade thought Jeff was cute, and it was me, Krista, whom he was asking to be his partner. It was perfect. I could make some brownies. We could work on social studies, then we could just talk! We could —

My wonderful thoughts stopped. Tonight, I could not do anything except try to deal with feeding and caring for a brother who was a beetle. I also had to try to tell my mother long distance that her only son, who she probably loved better than her only daughter, had been reduced to a nearsighted bug. "Uhh, gee, Jeff," I said when I realized that he was looking at me waiting for an answer, "I would really like to be partners, really, really, but I'm not sure I can do it tonight."

"Oh, well, when will you know?"

When would I know? When would my brother turn back into a boy? Maybe if I just wished for it hard enough. Why had Jeff noticed me today of all days! "Well, I'm not sure. Maybe I could call you after school," I said.

Jeff smiled. He was so cute when he smiled. "Aw, that's okay; don't worry about it. I really need the extra-credit since I'm new, and I want to get it done tonight. I'll just get a different partner."

I wanted to shout no! I wanted to stop everything and ask Jeff to help me with this awful mess, but I didn't. I just tried not to look as miserable as I felt when Jeff leaned over and asked Karena Hartlander to be his partner. I sent dirty looks at her trying to make her say no, but of course, Karena smiled sweetly at Jeff and said that being partners sounded like a a terrific idea. She gloated the whole rest of the day.

Social studies turned into science, and Tyler got the hiccups. We were all quietly writing a report when I heard the first hic. It was kind of high and scratchy, but definitely loud enough to be heard. Miss Kendall looked up from her desk and listened carefully. "Krista, would you like to get a drink of water?"

"Uh . . . no, ma'am. I would not!" I said forcefully. Then there was another loud hic, and I blushed. I knew it was rude, but I didn't see how I could have left the room to get water with my desk still hiccupping away. Mrs. Kendall looked surprised and she frowned at me again, but she didn't say anymore. The hics continued, and the kids around me began to giggle. I got redder and redder, but I tried to move my body as if I were the one hiccuping. It wasn't easy since I never knew exactly when Tyler's hiccups were coming.

But no matter how embarrassing it was, the result was still better than having anyone examine the inside of my desk, so Tyler continued hiccupping, and I continued moving my head as if it were me. Finally, everyone looked down at their desks again, and as soon as they did, there was a huge belch. "Krista," Mrs. Kendall reprimanded sharply.

"It wasn't me, honest, it wasn't," I protested, but the class laughed. I looked over at Jason, and he had the nerve to wink at me.

Finally, the three o'clock bell rang. Never had I been so glad for a day to end and a weekend to begin. I just sat in my seat almost too tired to move. Michelle and Julia didn't wait for me or ask me to walk home with them. They were still pretty mad, and I guess I couldn't blame them. Maybe some day, I'd be able to explain. Then again . . . maybe it was better not to even try.

Pretty soon, everyone had left. There was nothing emptier than a fifth-grade room on a Friday afternoon so I gathered up my stuff, slung my backpack over my shoulder, and carefully picked up my bracelet box. "Come on, Tyler, let's go home!"

"Krista, who are you talking to?" I'd forgotten that Mrs. Kendall was still in the room, erasing the blackboard.

"Oh, uh, just myself," I replied.

"Krista, are you okay? You don't seem like yourself at all today."

"Yeah, I'm fine. Good-bye, Mrs. Kendall." As I left room 5-A, Tyler's voice piped up, "You could have said I was bugging you. See it would have been like a joke, get it Krista? See the joke is that I'm a bug, and I would bug you — "

"Tyler!" Why was it that even though he was a beetle he still had all of his dumb habits that drove me crazy, including his silly jokes that he had to explain.

I was almost out of school when I remembered that I had never given Tyler's teacher the note I'd worked so hard to write the night before. I walked back toward Tyler's room. When I got there, his teacher was just locking the door. I got out my note, and my hand shook as I handed it to her. "My brother . . ." I could feel my heart pound, as I felt her teacher eyes on me. I took a deep breath and started again. "This is a note from our baby-sitter to excuse Tyler because he is . . . he's not well."

The teacher took the note, but she didn't even open it. "Oh, tell Tyler to feel better and that we missed him today." She glanced at her watch. "I'll never make my appointment on time." Then Tyler's teacher stuck the unopened note in her pocket and hurried off. Over her shoulder, she called, "Thank you for stopping to tell me about your brother. Have a nice weekend."

I shook my head. All that worrying about whether the note would look grown-up enough, and Tyler's teacher had never even opened it! I shook my head and walked out the front door of Horizon. Because no one was around, I took the lid off the box as I headed for home.

"Krista," came a wistful voice from inside the box, "if you see a good rock on the way home, would you kick it once for me?"

10

When I got home, I threw my backpack on the floor. The house was silent and empty. I put Tyler's box on the kitchen table, pulled out a chair, and sat down. It was so hard trying to be in charge and figure everything out. I was too tired and too defeated to enjoy the idea of being able to make myself a four-scoop hot-fudge sundae knowing I would not get in trouble for it.

"Krista." Tyler's voice sounded even farther away than it had before. "I don't feel so good."

"Me, either," I sighed. "I'm tired; my friends are mad at me, my teacher is mad at me, Jason made fun of me — it was just a swell day."

"Krista, I really don't feel good, and I'm scared."

I walked over to the box and peered in. He still looked exactly the same — like a very ugly black beetle. "What's the matter, Tyler?"

"I dunno. I feel like I'm getting sort of all stiff or something. It's weird."

I smiled. "No, it's not weird, it's great. I'll bet the spell is wearing off. I think you must be about to turn back into yourself. Oh Tyler." I bit my lip with pride. "I think we did it. I think we waited it out all by ourselves, and no one will ever know that you were a beetle."

Tyler seemed a little confused. "But I really was a beetle, right?"

Peering into the box, I said, "Tyler, you still are a beetle, but I don't think it's going to last much longer at all." Gone were all my thoughts of calling Mom, of giving up. I was old enough to have taken care of a real disastrous situation all by myself. I didn't think many, if any at all, of the grown-ups would know what to do if a member of the family turned into a bug.

For the next hour I sat at that box, and I stared at the beetle. Every little movement, every little antenna swish, I was sure was the beginning of the change. Every five minutes, I would ask Tyler how he was and if he felt any stiffer, any bigger. But each time, Tyler would reply that he just didn't feel good. Finally, the clock read 6 P.M., and I had to face the truth; my brother was not turning back into a person; he was going to stay a beetle.

It was time to give up and call Mom. I can't exactly describe what I felt like as I walked to the phone. Part of me was going to be so relieved to turn over all this mess to Mom, to have her come home and take care of me and Tyler. But part of me was dreading the conversation even more than the time when I was seven and I had to confess that I had been playing dress up with Mom's good makeup. I knew it was forbidden, but I figured I could be very careful, and everything would be fine. How could I know that Tyler, who was a pain even when he was only three, would take a tube of her favorite lipstick and color her ivory bedspread bright red? When I saw it, I was so scared and so mad at him, that I grabbed the lipstick and colored Tyler with it. Mom came in, looked at Tyler and her bed, and it was not a fun time from there.

Still, I headed for the phone. No matter how tough this was going to be, I needed my mom back. Just as I was about to put my hand on the receiver, the phone rang. It scared me and I jumped before carefully picking up the telephone. "Hello?"

"Krista, sweetheart, it's so good to hear your voice!"

"Mom," I croaked in disbelief, "it's really great to hear your voice, too. I — "

Before I could get any further, Mom interrupted me. "Krista, the most wonderful thing has happened. Yesterday, when I was getting this account straightened out, I had to go to a small town nearby. I met a gentleman who was vacationing there and it turns out that he is a buyer for a large chain of stores, and he was so impressed with our company's line of merchandise that he opened a huge, new account! Krista, do you know what this means?" Mom's voice just bubbled with enthusiasm. I couldn't remember ever hearing her this excited. "It means I'll be the high salesperson in our office. I may even get a promotion, and I'll definitely get a big bonus. Honey, that means we're all going to California. We'll be able to afford that vacation at the beach!" Mom went on and on about all the wonderful things this new account would mean to her and to us. Then she said, "Honey, it's so hectic. I have to leave right away for a meeting, but I'll be home tomorrow night." I heard her talking to someone else in the room. "Krista, I really wanted to talk to Mrs. Pickle-Nickle and to Tyler, but I've just got to leave. My new client and his secretary are waiting for me. I really don't want to blow this deal, and I don't quite have it closed yet. But before I hang up, I just want to check. Is Mrs. Pickle-Nickle managing all right; is everything okay at home?"

The words hung in my heart. With everything in me, I wanted to shout, "No everything is just terrible. It's worse than you could ever imagine. You've got to come home." I looked at the beetle box, and I thought about my mom's words. Before today, she had never talked about herself or her work first. She always had to hear all about us and our day. All of a sudden, I thought about Mom being a regular person instead of just our mom. She worked so hard, and if I told her the truth about what was happening here, she'd come home right away, but she would lose everything she had been so proud of. I took a deep breath, and then I did the most grown-up thing I've ever done in my whole life. I forced myself to be cheerful, and said, "Mom, everything is fine here. Tyler and I are real proud of you. Don't worry about us. We'll see you tomorrow night."

Mom laughed, "Oh, Krista, that's my girl. You sound so grown-up. I love you and Tyler more than anything. See you tomorrow!"

The line went dead. I tried to tell myself that it was only one more day. I tried to tell myself that a day didn't matter, but I hung up the phone, and then I just couldn't help it. I put my head in my hands and had a really good cry.

When I could finally stop crying, I explained to Tyler what had happened. He didn't even cry. He barely moved. I guess he felt even worse than I did. We didn't even feel like sundaes for dinner. I opened a can of soup, heated it in the microwave, poured a little into a milk cap for Tyler, and that was dinner for both of us.

After dinner, I turned on the TV. I could finally watch whatever I wanted, and Tyler couldn't get me in trouble, and Mom couldn't tell me to turn off the set. I took Tyler out of his box, and put him on the coffee table. Then I pulled the coffee table real close to the TV. Tyler said he still really couldn't see the picture, but he didn't much care. The funny thing was that neither did I. We just sort of sat there like two zombies until we finally trudged off to bed for the night. Once again, my little brother rested in a box on my desk in the glow of my Little Mermaid night-light.

When we got up on Saturday, I kept thinking that we just had to get through this one day, and then Mom would be home. Tyler said that he couldn't stand being in the house anymore. "Please," he begged, "let's at least go outside where it's sunny." Once we were in the backyard, I had to admit that the sun did feel good. I put Tyler's box down on the grass, and I stretched out next to it.

"Hey!" he called. "I don't wanna be in this dumb box anymore! Let me out on the grass."

"Tyler! Don't we have enough problems without you getting lost in the grass?"

"No fair!" he whined. "I'm not gonna get lost. Quit treating me like such a baby!"

"I'm not!" I said through gritted teeth. "I'm treating you like a bug!"

"Fine!" Tyler replied. "Then I'll just be a flying bug, and I'll fly right out of this box. I am not staying in this thing anymore!"

I put my face close to the box to continue the argument. I reminded him that he could get lost or killed if he tried to fly. He told me that I was just enjoying bossing him around every minute. He complained that I just didn't want him to have any fun.

That did it. I started yelling at him that he didn't appreciate anything. Maybe it was because I was so involved in fighting with my buggy brother that I didn't see it coming. But all of a sudden, Jason had hopped the back fence and was standing right in front of me.

I sat up immediately. "What the . . . ?"

"Ah, how cute. Krista talks to boxes now. Wait till I tell everyone on Monday. Krista spends her weekends yelling that the box isn't fair."

My face turned so red that I thought it was going to burn up. "I'm . . . I'm not talking to a box . . ." I stuttered.

"Hmm, then you must be talking to what's in the box." And before I could stop him, Jason reached down, scooped up the box, and looked inside. "How sweet, Krista has a pet beetle bug. Hmmm, I think I'll just feed him to my cat." And with that Jason sprinted back to the wall, the box still in his hand.

"Stop! Wait! You can't do that!" I yelled. But Jason either didn't hear me or decided just to ignore me as he hopped the fence back over into his own yard. For a minute, I was too stunned to move. Then the full impact of what Jason had said pulled me to my feet. Jason was going to give Tyler to his cat — only he didn't know it was Tyler. And Jason would definitely think it was pretty funny to feed what he thought was my pet beetle to his cat. I ran to the wall and looked over it, but Jason was no longer in his backyard. Poor Tyler! I just had to be in time to stop Jason. As fast as I could, I rushed through the gate at my house and ran next door. I rang the doorbell over and over again, and when no one answered, I began to scream, "Jason, open the door. This isn't a joke. Really, you're gonna kill someone. Please open the door fast!"

After what seemed like forever, a grinning Jason opened the door. "Why, it's Krista. I'll bet you've come to thank me for getting rid of your buggy problem!"

"What did you do to him! I want him back right now!" I was crying.

Jason's smile began to fade. "Him? Hey, take it easy. It was just a beetle — you know, a dumb little black bug that crawls on the ground. I didn't mean to make you cry. Look, it was all just one big joke. Stop crying, and I'll . . . I'll go find you some other beetle bug."

I began to cry even harder, and through my sobs, burst the words, "It wasn't just some beetle bug. IT WAS MY BROTHER!" Jason looked at me as if I were nuts, and I sobbed, "Don't you see, that bug was not just a bug. . . . It was Tyler!"

11

Jason looked confused and his face turned sort of white. "You really think that beetle in the box was your brother?"

I gulped. "Yes, I know it."

"Krista, maybe . . . maybe you should just come in for a few minutes, and I'll get you a drink of water or something."

The tears were rolling down my cheeks and splashing onto my sweatshirt. "I don't want a glass of water. I just want my brother."

"Okay . . ." Jason was looking at me as if he were dealing with a crazy person. "And you're telling me that your brother is a beetle."

I sniffed and nodded yes.

"Krista, is this some kind of a joke?"

I began to cry even harder. "Why do you think everything is a joke?"

Jason looked at me, bit his lip, and said, "Okay, Krista, please stop crying. I didn't feed your beetle to my cat. I don't even know where the cat is. I just dumped the beetle out on the lawn in my backyard. Stop crying, and we'll go see if we can find it. Come on."

I knew Jason didn't believe one word of what I had said about the beetle being Tyler and all, but at least Tyler wasn't in the cat's stomach. I was almost afraid to let myself hope that Tyler was somehow still okay. As we started out to Jason's backyard, he kept looking at me strangely, and then he said, "Uh . . . does your mom know that you think your brother is a beetle?"

"My mom is out of town, and it isn't that I *think* Tyler is a beetle. Tyler is a beetle. He just really *IS* a beetle." It was all too much to even begin to explain. "Just find him," I pleaded. "Then you'll understand."

Jason let out a big sigh. He was probably going to tell the whole school about this. I would be the school joke for years and years. I didn't even care. I just wanted Tyler to be okay. I got down on my hands and knees and I began to crawl carefully through the lawn, calling, "Tyler, Tyler . . ." but no one answered. I crawled forward a little bit, and when I looked up, I saw Jason still standing in one corner of his yard. His mouth was open, and he was staring at me. "Hey, I thought you were going to help me," I said.

Jason shook his head again and got down on his

knees. "Uh, Krista, how exactly is this bug going to answer you?"

"With his voice. Come on, Jason. Help me before something terrible happens to Tyler — if it hasn't already."

Jason got down on his knees and looked at the grass. "Tyler?" he asked more than called. Jason had barely even moved, when he yelled, "Wait just a minute!"

"You found him!" I called back excitedly.

"Okay. Where are your friends? Did you bet 'em that you could make me crawl and call out your brother's name? Well you win. Come on, tell Michelle and whoever else is around to come on out."

My brown eyes locked into Jason's. "What are you talking about?"

He wiped his hands on his jeans. "Krista, I just remembered science when Mrs. Kendall said that bugs don't have voice boxes like ours. How's Tyler gonna talk to us without a voice box? Come on, is he hiding, too."

"Nope! I'm not hiding. I'm right here!"

"Tyler!" I screamed. "You're okay! You're right where?"

"Just sit down real still right where you are, and put your hand out. Let's see if I can fly onto it! Ready . . . Oh, Krista. This is so much fun. You'd just love flying."

I put my hand out and waited. Jason came over behind me. I waited some more, but there was no Tyler. "Tyler's voice isn't all high and squeaky like that. It's your friends, isn't it," Jason fumed.

Then, suddenly I felt something tickle the palm of my hand. I grinned. "Tyler! You're okay!"

"Yep!" he replied. "Sorry, I missed your hand the first time I flew over here. I can't see so good, and these antennae, I don't really understand, but wow, my wings, I just love."

Jason took one look at Tyler and sank down on the grass. "Krista, I give. I'll never play another joke on you. I'll never even tease you at school anymore. You're the best joker I've ever seen. I could never ever even think of something like this, and even if I did, I could never make it all work. Just do me one huge favor. Don't tell everyone at school."

I tried not to smile. It was amazing how things worked out sometimes. Instead of Jason telling the whole school about me, he was asking me not to tell about him. Even better, Tyler was safe, and our secret was still a complete secret. I was just about to tell Jason he had a deal and walk proudly home when Tyler's voice piped up, "Oh, Jason, she didn't think this up. I really am a beetle. Our baby-sitter, who turned out to be an alien, turned me into this dumb bug right before she disappeared. It's been a terrible time, until you came and threw me out of my box, and I got to fly. Flying is just awesome!"

Jason moved right in front of me. He crossed his legs, and stared me right in the face. His blue eyes practically drilled holes into my head. For a minute it was real quiet, then Jason said, "I don't believe this. It can't be true. But it also can't be true that you made up a plan this crazy and had it all work. I've lived next door to you since we were in the second grade, and you never do crazy jokes like this." He sighed. "I just can't figure this one out."

Well, I certainly wasn't going to help him. I stood up with Tyler still on my outstretched hand, and I whispered, "Don't you dare fly away!" I started to walk back toward my own house. In a dumb sort of way, I almost hated to leave. It was easier to have someone else there, even if it was obnoxious old Jason. But I told myself it was only about ten hours until Mom came home. Boy, it would be good to see her. She'd straighten this mess out — that is, if Tyler was still here at all by then.

I was almost to the gate of Jason's backyard, when he said, "Wait up." I stood exactly where I was, and Jason came toward me. "Hey, listen, this is probably dumb, and if it is, you'll have one more thing to tell your friends, but if something is really wrong here, maybe I could help you?"

I should have kept walking out the gate. I don't know why I didn't or maybe I did, but I said, "Jason, where is Tyler?"

He looked at me, took a deep breath, and said, "On your hand?"

"Do you believe that?" I asked.

"It's really true," came Tyler's scratchy voice. "Please, Jason, we need your help."

Jason stuck his hand in his jeans pocket. "Okay, I believe it. It's crazy. It makes no sense at all, but I do believe it. Now, tell me what's going on."

"It's kind of a long, weird story." We walked over to Jason's picnic table. I put Tyler on the tabletop. Jason and I sat down, and I told him the entire story. Tyler piped in every so often to add a detail or two or talk about how boring it had been to spend a day in my class in a box. Jason's eyes just kept getting bigger, and he must have said "This is unreal" about ten times, but he listened really hard.

Finally I had told the whole story, and I added, "I feel real bad for Mom. She's gonna come home and be so happy about her job and everything, and we're going to have to tell her that her son is a beetle, and we have no idea when he'll be a boy again. I wish we could get Tyler back before she gets home. I mean, if you could've heard her on the phone. I've never heard my mom like that before."

"Hey, I'm thirsty!" Tyler interrupted.

"We'll get you water, just don't take off again," I ordered. We left Tyler on the table and picked a tulip from the garden to use as a water container. While Jason and I were putting the water in the flower, I whispered to Jason, "As long as I'm telling you everything, you might as well know one more thing. The reason I wish I could get Tyler back to being himself is that I don't think beetles live a real long time, and I don't know how much longer Tyler has. I'm not sure he'll even be alive by the time Mom gets home."

"Wow," Jason replied. "Well, then we've got to do something right now!"

"Like what?"

"Like" — Jason thought — "like, we'll go to that baby-sitting agency, and maybe we'll find Mrs. whoever she is."

"It's Mrs. Pickle-Nickle, and I told you that she's gone back to whatever planet she lived on. How can the baby-sitting agency help us?"

Jason paced back and forth, and Tyler called, "Hey, watch out. I'm coming to you. I'll get my own water. You guys take too long." Tyler missed us and landed in the grass somewhere, and we had to track him down.

"Tyler!" I scolded, "we can't spend all day looking for you and still get anything else done." Jason was on my side, and he went in his house, brought back his bug-keeper jar, and we plopped Tyler in it. My brother was furious, but there just wasn't time to argue.

"Come on," Jason said. "Even if Mrs. Pickle-Nickle isn't at that agency, maybe some of her alien friends are. And maybe one of them knows a way to undo that spell."

I had to admit that I hadn't thought of that. It was a long shot, but it wasn't any crazier than getting an alien for a baby-sitter or a beetle for a brother. Jason's mom wasn't home, and I wasn't sure how we could get to the baby-sitting agency since it was way across the city, but Jason said we'd figure something out. Ten minutes later, we had pooled all our money, and after calling a cab company to ask how much it would be to get from our house to 15 West Roosevelt, we had told the cab to come.

"Jason," I asked while we were waiting, "you ever been in a cab before by yourself?"

"Nope — have you?"

"Uh-uh," I said. "I hope this will be okay."

"Me, too," came a small scratchy voice. "I've

never been in a cab before with anybody. I've never been in a cab at all. Maybe our driver will be a cowboy, no a monster. What a day. First, I got to fly. Now I get to ride in a cab."

I saw the yellow car turn onto our street, and I wished I could share some of Tyler's excitement about it. For some reason, I had a real nervous sort of feeling in my stomach, like I hoped we weren't about to do something that was going to make everything worse. I looked at Jason standing next to me. He was trying to be real calm, but I could see that he was nervous, too. He'd even chipped in the five dollars he'd been saving for his new baseball glove so we'd have enough cab money. I looked at him again. It was so weird. Jason was the last person on earth I would have picked to share this terrible secret, and yet, somehow, I was glad he was here with me. Before I had time to think about that anymore, the cab pulled up in front of my house, stopped, and the driver got out.

"Who called a cab here?" came his gruff, low voice.

"We did," Jason said, but his voice shook a little.

"Are you kids playing? Cuz I don't like it when kids waste my time."

"No sir," I found myself blurting. "We are not playing; we are paying for you to take us to Fifteen West Roosevelt, and here's our money." I opened my purse, into which we had thrown all the change we could find.

The cabbie looked, shrugged, and said, "Well, then get in. What're we waiting for?"

12

We got in the backseat of the cab, and the driver made a U-turn and took off. "Hey, at least put me up at the window so I can sort of see," came a small voice.

The cab driver glared into his rearview mirror. "Somebody say something back there?"

"Uh, I was just wondering how long the ride will be, that's all," I said. I put the jar up close to the window and whispered for Tyler to be quiet. The cab rolled along, taking us further and further from any of our familiar landmarks. Pretty soon, I had no idea where we were, and I was sure Jason didn't either. Just as I began to think that maybe we were lost or maybe the cab driver hadn't understood where we wanted to go, or . . . the cab stopped.

"That'll be eleven dollars and eighty cents," the cabbie said, pointing to the figures on the little box in the front seat.

I looked around for The Nanny Agency, and I

saw a white building with blue awnings with THE NANNY AGENCY, NANNIES ARE NICE written on them. I opened my purse, and Jason and I counted out $11.80. A lot of it was in quarters and dimes, and the driver looked at our hands filled with change. "Are you kiddin' me? I'm supposed to count all that?"

"Well, you don't have to," Jason said. "I got an *A* in math, and I'm sure it's right."

"You kids ever hear of a tip?" the cabbie sighed.

"Listen," Jason said, and I noticed that he sat up very straight and folded his arms across his chest. "Your sign says eleven dollars and eighty cents. We have eleven dollars and eighty cents. Do you want it or not?"

A minute later the cab roared off with our money. Jason and I stood on the corner and stared at The Nanny Agency across the street. "So, now that we're here . . . what are we gonna tell them?" I asked. I definitely did not think that we should tell them the truth. All of a sudden, I wished I had taken the time to change out of my grubby old jeans and sweatshirt and into my good clothes.

Jason stared at The Nanny Agency sign. "Do you think maybe they're all aliens there?"

I told Jason that I didn't think so because Mrs. Pickle-Nickle had sounded like she'd picked out this particular agency after she had come to

Earth. We tried and tried to think of exactly what to say, but we couldn't come up with one good idea. Finally, Jason said, "Well, I got us here, but I think that's as far as I can get us!"

Since I had no idea what it would be like in The Nanny Agency, I figured we would just have to see what happened. So without any real plan, we finally crossed the street and went into the agency. A little bell tinkled when we walked through the door. I half expected a sweet-looking little granny to meet us, but a woman in a dark blue suit was sitting at a desk. "May I help you?" she asked. The woman got up from her desk and came toward us. "We don't often get children in here. This is a training and placement agency for people who want to take care of children."

"Oh, we know that!" Jason said quickly.

"I see," said the lady. "No, actually, I don't see. What is that you two children want?"

Looking very unsure, Jason turned toward me. The lady was staring at us, and I knew I had to say something. "Uhh, well, my name is Krista, and uh, this is my brother . . . " I caught myself because I had been about to point to the jar and say "Tyler," but at the last minute I said, "Jason." And I pointed to him.

The woman smiled and stuck out her hand. "Well, it's nice to meet you both. My name is Mrs.

Marsple, and I would like to talk, but I really do have a lot of work to do, so if you don't need anything special maybe you children should run along."

I knew I had to do something fast. We had used up Jason's baseball glove money and my Chanukah money on cab fare, and it couldn't all be for nothing. "Well, really," I said, shifting the bug jar in my hand, "we came because we wanted to know about getting a baby-sitter."

The woman looked amused. "You want to hire a baby-sitter?"

"Yeah," I replied, my plan taking shape. "You see we live next door to two kids, their names are Krista and Tyler, and they had the neatest baby-sitter. Her name was Mrs. Pickle-Nickle." I took a deep breath and watched Mrs. Marsple's face real carefully to see how she would react.

"Mrs. Pickle-Nickle . . . oh, yes, she's new. She's just graduated, but she is a lovely lady, and she looks like the perfect grandmother."

"Yes, have you seen her lately?" Jason blurted.

Mrs. Marsple looked confused. "Have I seen her? Isn't she baby-sitting your friends?"

I shot at look at Jason. "Sure, she is," I lied. "We just want to know if there are any other baby-sitters just like her?"

Mrs. Marsple smiled, "Well, I think you'll find

that all our sitters are qualified, caring, and competent. In fact, that's our motto. Listen, children, I think it's really sweet that you came here, and I'll certainly pass along your compliment to Mrs. Pickle-Nickle, or you can go next door and tell her yourselves how much you like her. I've really got to get back to work now. Here's our agency card. You just give this to your parents and have them call us. We'll get you a wonderful sitter. I guarantee it."

This was getting nowhere fast. Obviously, Mrs. Marsple didn't know that Mrs. Pickle-Nickle had deserted us, and I was pretty sure she had no idea that Mrs. Pickle-Nickle was an alien. We trudged out of The Nanny Agency before Mrs. Marsple could start asking questions about our parents and why we were there without them.

"Well, that pretty well bombed, huh?" Jason said as we walked.

"Yeah, it did." I felt bad for me, bad for Tyler, and even bad for Jason. After all, he didn't have to be part of this at all. "Hey, Jason, thanks for trying. We'd better find a phone and call a cab to come get us."

"Wait. Watch this." To my surprise, I saw Jason put his finger to his lips, whistle a piercing whistle, and then wave his arms at a cab going the other way. The cabbie made a U-turn in the middle of the street and pulled up in front of us. "Pretty good, huh?" Jason said proudly. "I saw it in a movie. That's how I knew it would work."

We got in the cab and told the driver our address. In the backseat, Jason was still feeling pretty proud of himself. He nudged me, "So I'm your brother, huh?"

Geez, Tyler AND Jason for brothers — what a nightmare that would be. Speaking of Tyler, I looked at the jar. He'd been real quiet for a long time. "Hey, Tyler," I whispered softly, "you okay in there?"

"I don't think so. I feel real tired. It's even too hard to move around." Tyler's voice sounded real weak.

"Tyler, hang in there!" I said. "You're probably just hungry or thirsty or something."

"Naw, I don't want anything."

"Tyler, it's probably the jar. That's what it is. I'll get you out, and you'll be fine. You'll see." My heart was starting to pound.

"Okay, kids, this the place?" I had been so busy with Tyler that I hadn't even noticed we were home again. We paid the cabbie and got out of the car.

"Jason, I think something may be really wrong with Tyler." I was biting my lip, but I could feel that tears were going to start.

Jason took the jar from me, and twisted the lid trying to get it open. Finally the lid came loose, and I put the jar on its side. "Come on, Tyler, just crawl out on my hand," I pleaded.

But Tyler didn't move and he didn't speak.

13

Jason picked up the jar. "Come on, let's take Tyler in your house. We'll take him out of the jar. We'll give him some food and some water, and he'll be okay." I followed Jason as he carried the jar to the house. Maybe, the lid was too tight. Maybe Tyler couldn't breathe. We got inside, and turned the jar sideways on the kitchen table. I filled up a milk cap with some milk, and I got a potato chip and crushed it. I put everything right near the opening of the jar.

"Come on, Tyler," I pleaded. "It's just a little walk. There's really good food and milk. Just come out of the jar."

"Can't . . . ," his weak voice finally replied, "too far."

Really scared, I scrunched my hand as small as I could and stuck it into the jar. Cupping Tyler inside, I gently began to pull my hand out of the jar until I had Tyler sitting on the kitchen table right next to the milk. "Tyler, if you could just take some milk, you would feel better. Please, Tyler, try!"

Tyler did try, but after one sip, he said he was just too tired and that he couldn't do it. His voice sounded real faint and soft, and then he said, "Hey, Krista, I'm sorry I made you so mad all the time. You were a pretty good sister."

"Tyler," I shouted, "don't you do this. I still am your sister, and we have lots more fights to fight, and lots more stuff to do, and — " I stopped because I didn't think Tyler could hear me. He was very still.

Looking at the motionless beetle as if somehow I could almost will it to move, I said to Jason, "I never should have waited to tell Mom. I never should have thought I was old enough to handle everything on my own. I — "

"Holy gazonkers!" Jason interrupted me. "Who . . . what . . .?"

There was a bright yellow spot in the corner of the kitchen. Then there was a strange smell. A weird-looking head and body began to take shape. I could hear Jason's sharp gasp as the figure began to appear. Neither one of us moved even so much as an inch. The figure continued to grow, but in the bright yellow light, it was hard to see exactly what was happening; and then all at once, the glow was gone, and standing before us, in all her innocent grandmotherly look was none other than Mrs. Pickle-Nickle.

"I don't believe it," Jason gasped. He reached up and rubbed both his eyes real hard. "I won't believe it for as long as I ever live." He began to walk over to the figure, and he reached out almost as if daring himself to do so and pinched her arm.

"Ouch! I say, young man, that is not very nice behavior!"

"Very nice behavior?" I shouted at Mrs. Pickle-Nickle. "Look what you've done to my brother! *That's* not nice behavior." I was a little hysterical. "I think he's dead. How could you have turned him into a beetle and then just left us here?"

Mrs. Pickle-Nickle wrung her hands. "Oh dear, that is exactly what my superiors said. They were very angry, very, very angry, with me and they said I had to return here to make things right." Her double chins bobbed as if to emphasize her point. Then she pursed her lips unhappily. "Only, you see, no one could figure out how to break the spell. Oh, it isn't as if they haven't been working. They know that beetles have very short life spans. That's why how to undo what I did to your brother has been the major topic of concern of the Zxieocm executive board. My land, I never expected to be at the center of all this controversy. It's just plumb worn me out. Earth is such a complicated — "

I interrupted, "But did they find something?"

Mrs. Pickle-Nickle pushed her granny glasses back up on her nose, but she wouldn't look at me. "Well . . . I think so. At least I certainly hope so. If this doesn't work, oh my gracious, I . . . I don't know what I'll do. I can't stay here, and if I fail, I don't dare go home." Almost more to herself than to me, she added, "Well, I suppose I might as well try it." With that, from her apron pocket, Mrs. Pickle-Nickle took a small, clear container filled with a yellowy kind of goop. It looked awful.

"Just what is that stuff, and what exactly are you going to do with it?" Jason asked.

But Mrs. Pickle-Nickle didn't answer. She walked over to Tyler, looked down at him, and shook her head. "I think you're a rather nice looking beetle. It certainly would have made things much easier if you'd thought so, too," she said; and then Mrs. Pickle-Nickle opened the container and dumped the yellow stuff all over him. Jason and I leaned toward Tyler. As bad as the goop looked, it smelled even worse. I held my breath, and I crossed my fingers. This just had to work!

14

I'm not sure how long we all stood frozen and staring, but finally, Jason said, "Uhh, maybe this just takes some time — like an hour or something, right?" Mrs. Pickle-Nickle didn't answer, and Jason added, "Maybe, you're supposed to say something besides 'hmmm.' Don't you have some magic words or something?"

I could feel my eyes start to sting with tears. My brother was still not moving, and now he was covered with some awful goop. Mrs. Pickle-Nickle wrung her hands again. "Oh, dear. Oh, dear. Oh, dear. I am so very sorry. You must believe that. I really didn't mean to make such a mess of things, and I did come back to try to make everything right. Can't you at least say that I tried?"

Jason and I both looked at Mrs. Pickle-Nickle. Trying wasn't good enough. How could trying get me back my little brother! In all the ways, in all the times I had dreamed of his just disappearing and leaving me alone, I had never wished for anything like this. I glared at Mrs. Pickle-Nickle. Didn't she know that she was supposed to be a grown-up if she was going to take care of kids?! "What good did it do for you to come back if you couldn't fix anything at all?! Any grown-up would have known better than to turn a kid into a beetle in the first place."

Mrs. Pickle-Nickle tapped her black boot and replied, "Now, wait just a minute. I would never have made any changes in Tyler if you and he both hadn't wished for the changes to happen. Did you forget that? This disaster is not entirely my responsibility, you know." My heart ached because I knew what she said was true, but still, I hadn't really meant for anything terrible to happen to Tyler.

Mrs. Pickle-Nickle began pacing back and forth. "Look, no one meant for my visit to be so sad. I became an Earth baby-sitter to make children happy." Then suddenly, Mrs. Pickle-Nickle smiled and said, "I know. I'll make you some chocolate chip cookies. You liked those."

"Mrs. Pickle-Nickle, I don't want any chocolate chip cookies. I just want my little brother. How can you be so . . . how can you even begin to think that some dumb chocolate chip cookies can make anything better?"

For the first time since she had arrived today, Mrs. Pickle-Nickle took off her granny glasses and looked me straight in the eye. I didn't know why I hadn't noticed the yellow rings in her eyes the first time I'd met her. If I had, maybe I'd have known she was an alien or something.

She put one chubby hand on my shoulder. "Krista, I know you want your brother back. I want him back, too, more than anything. Everyone on my planet tried their very hardest to reverse what I did, but no one has ever had to undo turning a human into a beetle. I guess the formula was wrong . . . or the beetle itself just couldn't live long enough. I'm trying to think that at least your brother got to have a grand adventure. He got to see life as no other Earth person ever has, and I know that because of what I did, even though I did it trying to make you happy, neither of our lives will ever be the same. I do understand that. I know that I'm going back to face punishment on my planet, and you — " Mrs. Pickle-Nickle stopped and bit her lip. Then she said, "So even though I know making chocolate chip cookies won't make things right, I'm going to do it. We're all going to sit down and have some and remember good things about Tyler. And then we're both going to face what we have to face."

With that I watched Mrs. Pickle-Nickle put together the dough ingredients and drop spoonfuls on a cookie sheet. Neither Jason nor I said anything at all, and both of us stared at Mrs. Pickle-

Nickle because I don't think either of us could stand the idea of looking at the kitchen table and the little bug lying so still on it. Mrs. Pickle-Nickle put the cookies in the oven in complete silence and stood by the oven door with her arms folded against her apron. She stared off into space, and I thought that behind those granny glasses, I saw tears in her eyes. The room was so quiet that I could even hear the second hand moving around the clock on the wall.

"Boy, does something ever smell good!" The voice . . . it sounded familiar. It sounded almost like . . . I turned toward the table. "Tyler!" I screamed with delight as a blond-headed little boy sat in the middle of the kitchen table and rubbed his eyes.

"Holy gazonkers, this is . . . this is . . . it's unbelievable!" Jason shouted.

I ran back to the kitchen table, and I threw my arms around Tyler. "Are you okay? Please say you're okay." I let go of my regular-sized brother just a minute so I could look at him and make myself believe he was really all there.

"Well . . . I'm real hungry, and I think it's real weird that I'm sitting in the middle of the kitchen table." And then he noticed Jason. "And it's even weirder that you invited Jason over for cookies when you can't stand him." Tyler scratched his head. He looked like himself; he sounded okay, even if he didn't seem to remember anything. I threw my arms around him again and hugged him for all he was worth. I wasn't sure I was ever letting go of him. I was laughing because I was so relieved, and I guess that's why I didn't hear the door open.

"Mrs. Pickle-Nickle, you truly are a miracle worker!"

I turned around. "Mom!" I called.

"Hi kids, hi Jason. My goodness, what a wonderful treat to walk in the door and see you hugging your brother instead of the two of you fighting. And how nice of you to invite Jason over." Then she looked at Tyler for a minute, "Honey, why are you sitting on the table?"

"Uhh, I'm not sure, Mom. I'll just get down."

Mom walked over and hugged us both. "Oh, you look wonderful. It's so good to be home. Oh, and Mrs. Pickle-Nickle, those cookies smell divine."

"Thank you, ma'am, it's my own special recipe."

I thought to myself that Mom should only know about Mrs. Pickle-Nickle's other special recipes. I looked at Jason, and he looked back at me, but Mom didn't notice as she continued speaking to Mrs. Pickle-Nickle. "I just can't thank you enough. This has been the perfect ending to a very successful trip. To come home and find my children so happy and together — they do have a tendency to fight, as you've probably seen. It drives me crazy, and other sitters have complained, but this . . . this is wonderful."

"Well, thank you, ma'am. They're very interesting children. Excuse me a moment."

I thought uh-oh, this is it; this is when Mrs. Pickle-Nickle is going to disappear into a yellow-blob alien, and just wait until Mom sees that! But Mrs. Pickle-Nickle didn't disappear at all. She just turned, put on the oven mitt, and pulled out luscious-looking chocolate chip cookies.

"My . . . ," Mom said, "those not only smell wonderful, they look perfect! Tyler and Krista, you're really lucky to have had Mrs. Pickle-Nickle here as your sitter." Then she turned to Mrs. Pickle-Nickle. "Well, I don't want to keep you any longer. I'm sure you have things to do. Let me pay you."

"Oh, that's all right, ma'am. You needn't pay me at all."

Mom laughed. "Don't be silly. I'm going to request you any time I need a sitter from now on, and I absolutely wouldn't feel right about that if I couldn't pay you."

My mouth dropped open. Mrs. Pickle-Nickle looked doubtfully at me, but Mom didn't notice. Mrs. Pickle-Nickle only said, "Uh . . . actually, I don't think I'll be available much, and I'm just glad things turned out so well this time. Trust me. You don't need to pay me."

But Mom insisted on paying Mrs. Pickle-Nickle, and took out her checkbook. Mrs. Pickle-Nickle said, "Well, all right, if you must, ma'am, but if so, I'd prefer being paid in cash."

At first, Mom seemed surprised and said she wasn't even sure she had that much cash in her purse, but she dug around, and finally, she placed a bunch of bills in Mrs. Pickle-Nickle's hand. Then she said, "Thank you so much again. I've never come home before to find my children hugging each other, and I'm delighted that Krista's become friendlier with Jason. I'll definitely request you again from the agency. Do you need me to take you home or will you be calling a cab?"

"Oh, I've got transportation," Mrs. Pickle-Nickle replied.

Mom smiled again and shook Mrs. Pickle-Nickle's hand. "It's been a pleasure to have you here. Now if you don't mind, I'll let the children say good-bye to you, and I'll go upstairs to unpack. Kids, come on up after Mrs. Pickle-Nickle leaves. You too, Jason."

Jason looked a little pale. "Uh, that's okay, Mrs. Klausner. I really should go home. I'll let you just see your kids. Krista, why don't you call me later."

I said I definitely would. Jason went home. Mom went upstairs. And there Tyler and I were in the kitchen, just us kids and Mrs. Pickle-Nickle. It seemed as if she had first arrived months ago instead of just days ago. Mrs. Pickle-Nickle's chubby rosy cheeks smiled, and she said, "Good-bye Krista. Good-bye Tyler. I learned a lot from you — like maybe it's better if people's wishes don't always come true. It's been quite an Earthly adventure, you know, but I don't think I'll be back. I will never forget the two of you, and I'm truly very sorry for the trouble I caused. Maybe this will help make it better." She put the money Mom had paid her in my hand. "I won't need this. You split it with your brother." Then Mrs. Pickle-Nickle reached out and hugged us both real tight. "Good-bye," she whispered, and when she pulled away from us, a bright yellow light began to fill the room, and then Mrs. Pickle-Nickle was gone.

"Wow!" Tyler said. "Did you see that? You know there's something real weird about that baby-sitter, huh?"

I didn't answer. I just looked at my little brother, his two arms, two legs, his blue eyes, and his head of blond hair, and I smiled.

Tyler looked at me, "How come you're smiling? What're you gonna do? I'll tell Mom! And hey! That baby-sitter gave you money. She said half of it was for me. I want my half."

I laughed out loud. Things were definitely back to normal. My brother was still a pest, but at least, he was no longer a dead bug! And Jason the jerk, whom I had never thought of as anything except a terrible tease, had turned out to be a real friend when I needed one most. I sat for a minute thinking about everything that had happened. Then I turned to Tyler, "You get one third of the money."

Tyler's blond hair fell into his eyes, and he pushed it back ready to fight. "No fair. That means you get more."

"No," I said, "you, Jason and I — we all get the same."

"Jason?" Tyler squeaked. "But you hate Jason even more than you hate me." Tyler looked at me suspiciously. "There's something sorta strange that happened here, right?"

I wasn't sure if Tyler would ever remember exactly what had happened, but I was sure that now was not the time to try to explain it all, so I just said, "You are always strange. Here's your share of the money. Now, come on, let's go see Mom! Even though I'm older, you can go up the stairs first."

"I can?" Tyler said. "Really?"

"Yeah, but just for tonight!"

Tyler scampered up the stairs. I watched him go, and after taking one long look out the kitchen window at the starry night, I softly said, "Goodbye, Mrs. Pickle-Nickle — good luck." Then I followed my little brother up the stairs.

About the Author

Terri Fields lives in Phoenix, Arizona, with her husband, Rick, and her children, Lori and Jeffrey. A teacher who believes there are always magical mysteries at home and in school, she's also the author of *The Day the Fifth Grade Disappeared*.

APPLE® PAPERBACKS

Pick an Apple and Polish Off Some Great Reading!

BEST-SELLING APPLE TITLES

❑ MT43944-8	**Afternoon of the Elves** Janet Taylor Lisle	**$2.75**
❑ MT43109-9	**Boys Are Yucko** Anna Grossnickle Hines	**$2.95**
❑ MT43473-X	**The Broccoli Tapes** Jan Slepian	**$2.95**
❑ MT40961-1	**Chocolate Covered Ants** Stephen Manes	**$2.95**
❑ MT45436-6	**Cousins** Virginia Hamilton	**$2.95**
❑ MT44036-5	**George Washington's Socks** Elvira Woodruff	**$2.95**
❑ MT45244-4	**Ghost Cadet** Elaine Marie Alphin	**$2.95**
❑ MT44351-8	**Help! I'm a Prisoner in the Library** Eth Clifford	**$2.95**
❑ MT43618-X	**Me and Katie (The Pest)** Ann M. Martin	**$2.95**
❑ MT43030-0	**Shoebag** Mary James	**$2.95**
❑ MT46075-7	**Sixth Grade Secrets** Louis Sachar	**$2.95**
❑ MT42882-9	**Sixth Grade Sleepover** Eve Bunting	**$2.95**
❑ MT41732-0	**Too Many Murphys** Colleen O'Shaughnessy McKenna	**$2.95**

Available wherever you buy books, or use this order form.

- -

Scholastic Inc., P.O. Box 7502, 2931 East McCarty Street, Jefferson City, MO 65102

Please send me the books I have checked above. I am enclosing $_____ (please add $2.00 to cover shipping and handling). Send check or money order — no cash or C.O.D.s please.

Name_____ Birthdate_____

Address _____

City_____ State/Zip _____

Please allow four to six weeks for delivery. Offer good in the U.S.A. only. Sorry, mail orders are not available to residents of Canada. Prices subject to change.

APP693